THE LONE RIDER

THE LONE RIDER

LEE MARTIN

VACA MOUNTAIN PRESS
VACAVILLE, CALIFORNIA, USA

Vaca Mountain Press
Paperback ISBN 13: 978-1-952380-29-7
Kindle ISBN 13: 978-1-952380-30-3

Also available in
Large Print ISBN 13: 978-1-952380-31-0

Library of Congress Catalog Card Number: 93-90134

Interior design by Eddie Vincent, ENC Graphic Services
Cover design by Christopher Wait for ENC Graphic Services
Cover images © Getty Images

Published by Vaca Mountain Press

Visit Lee Martin Westerns on Facebook.

To all of my wonderful family,
and in the fond memory of
my beloved mother,
my beautiful sister Arlene,
our rough riding brothers,
and for Jim Liontas.

THE LONE RIDER

ONE

ounging on his hard bunk in the jailhouse, unaware of the horror he was about to read, Zach Lassiter spread the newspaper on his knees while Pops, the jailer, made the coffee, cackling to himself as usual.

Wearing the badge of the town marshal of Lock's Ferry, Montana Territory, Zach was bored. The town was too peaceable. A big man in his early thirties with a square jaw and slightly crooked nose, ice-blue eyes, and curly black hair, he was getting mighty restless. The Cheyenne newspaper was six months old, but it was still news from out of town.

"Coffee's ready," Pops said.

Suddenly, Zach felt his mouth go dry. His stomach was a huge rock inside him. Eyes burning and brimming with sudden tears, he stared at the item on the second page. He could barely breathe as he read it over and over until he could see no more. He drew back, his heart cold in his big chest. His long fingers clutched and crumpled the edges of the paper.

Pops leaned forward. "You havin' some kind of attack?"

"Read this."

1

"You know I can't read."

Zach wiped his eyes with the back of his hand. He stared again at the article. He could barely hold the paper. His hands were weak, his fingers numb, and sweat covered his body.

"What is it, son?"

"Hanging down in Reata, New Mexico Territory. Six months ago."

"I've been through there. That's Scofield country. Levi Scofield, he's some kind of cattle king. Him and his sons, they's royalty down there."

"Says right here, vigilantes hanged my brother, Ricky Lassiter. Claimed he was a rustler."

Zach felt sick. He tried to sip his coffee, but his hand was shaking. It was a long while before he could compose himself, and he used the thick coffee to ease his dry mouth and throat. Tears trickled down his rough face.

Zach glanced at Pops, a kind old man whose obvious concern hit home, and he let his story spill forth because he couldn't stop the words.

"Ricky, he married Emily Swartz, a girl I was crazy about back in Kansas. Five years ago. I'd been working as a deputy marshal, but when she chose Ricky, I left town."

"Take it easy, son."

"I got a letter once, sayin' they was movin' to Reata. He was a gunsmith, always mindin' his own business, and here they went and hanged 'im. I know blamed well he was innocent. He weren't no rustler, I can tell you that."

"Zach, even if he was innocent, he's gone now, and if you head down to Scofield country and start mixin' in their business, someone's gonna cut you down. And your fancy reputation as a town tamer and gunfighter ain't gonna keep 'em from gettin' you in the back."

"You figure the Scofields were in on the lynchin'?"

"All I know is, not much happens around there unless Levi Scofield allows it. You show up down there, they'll know why. Even the sheriff could be in Levi's pocket."

Zach was in a hurry. First he turned in his badge, and then he bought supplies. Wearing a black, wide brimmed Stetson, his old leather vest pulled over a blue, double-breasted shirt, he packed his gear on his bay gelding. It was spring of 1880, and by late afternoon he was riding south through the green grass and sprinkled flowers of Wyoming Territory, watching for Sioux and haunted by the images of Ricky and Emily.

It was two weeks before he passed Santa Fe and followed the eastern bank of the sleepy Rio Grande into New Mexico Territory, then headed east across the tracks of the Denver & Rio Grande.

Camped along a whispering creek with a tiny campfire under the starry sky, Zach oiled his six-gun and heard Emily's laughter, her teasing voice.

"Oh, Zachariah, you tell such stories."

And Ricky's sad farewell. *"Don't forget us, Zach."*

After years of wearing a badge and earning a reputation, traveling the West in every direction, searching for he knew not what, Zach had failed to find a new life for himself. Days in the saddle and nights under the stars had been pretty lonesome, but he had survived.

Staring into the flickering flames of the campfire, he had never felt so alone. Lying back, he stared at the stars in the deep black sky, his heart beating something fierce. Everything in the heavens was glittering, and he knew the answers were up there, if he could only reach that far. He spoke softly.

"Lord, I know you ain't got much time for the likes of me, but if you was to point the way, I'd sure be obliged."

He closed his eyes, the chill of night on his burning face.

*   *   *

It was a Saturday morning when Zach reached Scofield country. Herds of cattle, whiteface, longhorns, and crossbreeds, roamed in all directions on the sea of waving grass. Naked bluffs were in the south beyond the treeless plain, and to the northwest, distant blue mountains were trimmed with snow.

Reaching another rise in the land, he reined up and gazed toward the distant town spreading on either side of the main trail to the south. Creeks crisscrossed the plains, and one deep-furrowed stream with a small wooden bridge marked the entrance to the main street from the southwest.

Zach pushed back his black Stetson and wiped his sweaty face with his bandanna, then pulled the hat back down over his forehead. His vest felt heavy and warm over his double-breasted shirt, but its pockets were useful.

As he rode down the slope, he saw two riders coming from the north. They were riding free as the wind as if to intercept him; they appeared to be cowhands, except that one had long, flame-colored hair flowing from under a white hat.

They hit the trail in front of him, blocking his path, and Zach reined to a halt. He casually pushed his hat back and leaned on the pommel to study them. The man was in his sixties with a face lined by weather and worry, his nose large and his voice thick.

"Howdy, stranger."

The woman was something else. Wearing a riding skirt, a man's white shirt, and a red bandanna, with a six-gun at her right hip and chinstrap holding her hat, she sat the saddle on her gray mare like a man. She looked to be in her early twenties.

And she was gorgeous, with peach-colored skin flushed by the sun, large dark-green eyes, and an air of practiced royalty. Her red hair was long and thick and glistening, blowing like red satin in the sunlight. Across her pert nose and high cheekbones was a sprinkle of pale freckles.

She took his breath away. He could barely tip his hat.

"I'm Oscar Wallace," the older man said. "Foreman on the Antler spread, where you're ridin'. We've had some rustlers around here, so we like to take a look at strangers. This here's Miss Sally Scofield. Her father and brothers, they own Antler."

"Zach Lassiter."

Wallace was stunned. "The gunfighter?"

But Sally was amused, her white teeth flashing. "Well, Mr. Lassiter, you surely do not look like a gunfighter. Where are your silver conchos and pearl-handled pistols? You should be wearing black. And gunfighters don't have curly hair."

Her voice was so musical and her impertinence so light, Zach found himself liking her immediately. She was flirting with him, and that was mighty hard to resist. He grinned at her.

"You wear that six-gun just for show?"

She drew herself up a little, but she was still smiling. "I'll match you any day, Mr. Lassiter."

"Now then," Wallace said. "You just passin' through?"

"Maybe."

"If you're lookin' for work, we can always use a man who can handle a gun. Rustlers been pickin' off the herd. And there's always a stray Mescalero. Forty a month."

Zach straightened, but hesitated. "Sorry, but I—"

"Double that," Sally said.

"I'll think on it."

Wallace seemed annoyed that she had thrown in a higher price, but Zach was right flattered. She seemed embarrassed that he didn't take her offer, and she frowned.

"I'll rest up in Reata," Zach said. "I'll let you know."

The foreman grunted. "Well, listen, when you're ready to talk serious, you come see me. Head due north, and you can't miss the ranch. Look for a red butte."

Sally flashed a smile and turned her mare around, digging in her heels and riding north with hair flying. She rode like a Comanche and looked to be one with her mount. Zach had never seen any woman so exciting, not even Emily, whose personality had been more sweet and gentle.

Wallace was still there, studying him.

"Don't be gettin' no ideas about Miss Scofield."

"Best lookin' woman I ever saw."

"Forget it. Meanwhile, Lassiter ain't no common name around these parts. You kin to Ricky Lassiter?"

"My brother."

"And you know what happened?"

"That's why I'm here."

"The sheriff never found the men what done it."

"Maybe he wasn't workin' very hard at it."

The foreman grunted. "His name's Jed Long, and if I were you, I sure wouldn't take that attitude."

"Where did it happen?"

"Coyote Creek, way east of town where there's some cottonwoods. Been a lot of rustling this last year or so. Some of the small ranchers been gettin' fed up and some been hiring gun hands. Could be some of their new boys just got the wrong idea and made a mistake. Everyone else knows your brother weren't no rustler."

"What about Scofield?"

"Well, they've lost more cattle than anyone. But the lynchin' was on the line between their grass and the Square T, run by Ray Tealman. Maybe you oughta talk to him."

"Maybe so. Is my brother's wife still in town?"

"Yeah, last I heard."

Zach tipped his hat and rode on toward town. He grew anxious as he neared. Seeing Emily would not be easy.

Reata was a typical cow town full of wagons, horses, mules, and the usual hands drifting in on Saturday. Stores and respectable establishments were on the north side of the street, and behind them were houses with white fences and some flowers. Paint was peeling from the sun, and roofs had been patched. Boardwalks had suffered the usual beating.

On the south side, saloons and dance halls with glittery windows were side by side. Behind them were shacks and tents. At the far end of town was the livery, with a tattered rope dangling from the timber extended out of the front window.

Across from the hotel and jailhouse, between two saloons, was Pete's Cafe. As Zach wolfed down some ham and eggs and heavy coffee, he was doing a lot of thinking. He was going to have to size up the sheriff right soon. If the law could be trusted, he'd have an easier time of it.

It was late afternoon when he crossed over to the sheriff's

office. As he started to reach for the door handle, the door swung open and a woman was standing there, wearing a black velvet jacket and skirt.

Zach caught his breath. She was in her mid-twenties, blond, lovely, with dark-brown eyes. She moved gracefully and smelled of lilacs.

But her face was familiar.

Devastated, Zach felt his throat go dry. He removed his hat slowly, his muscles nearly frozen, and he couldn't breathe.

Was it Emily?

TWO

Zach couldn't move as he stood in front of the jailhouse door. The woman in front of him was the woman he had loved and never forgotten. Sunlight caressed her fair skin as she closed the heavy door behind her.

He felt as if he were in limbo. The five years of separation had put a heavy lid on his emotions. And now, even as he stared at her and remembered, he felt only numb. His voice was low and sounded strange.

"Emily?"

Recognition darkened her face. "Zachariah?"

"I heard about Ricky only a short time ago. I came as fast as I could."

Tears filled her eyes as she swayed and sat down slowly on a bench in the shade. Zach stood near her, hat in hand, his stomach reeling. He was confused, frozen, as he stared down at her. After all, she had loved Ricky, not him.

"Oh, Zach, it was awful."

"Did you see it?"

"No, I was home waiting supper for him until after midnight.

Ricky had gone to deliver a rifle to the Tealman ranch, so I just decided he had stayed overnight, and I finally went to bed. The next day, the sheriff told me that vigilantes had hanged him in the middle of the night, way out by Coyote Creek."

"You got any idea who done it?"

"No, but they wrote 'rustler' in the dirt."

"And no one's been arrested for it?"

"No one."

Zach felt awkward and odd. "You gettin' along?"

"Yes, I sold the gun shop and the house. I live at the boardinghouse now. But I have enough to live comfortably."

"You and Ricky, did you have any kids?"

She shook her head as she stood up, and smiled at him.

"Zachariah, we've heard about you from time to time. All those gunfights. But you haven't changed in all these years."

"Older, maybe. Where's the boardinghouse?"

"Behind the hotel, several houses back. There's a sign, Ma Rindell's."

"Where's Ricky buried?"

"There's a cemetery behind the church, east of town."

He tipped his hat, wondering how five years could have gone by so fast, while now it seemed as if they were standing on her mother's front porch, passing the time of day.

She smiled at him and moved away down the boardwalk without looking back, swaying her hips the way he remembered. She had always had a funny laugh and twinkling eyes, but now she was a serious woman, someone different.

He watched her go into a store, and he turned to the door of the jailhouse. Zach swallowed hard, still shaken. It was a long moment before he went inside, closing the door behind him.

He could see a man sitting at a desk with his back to the rear wall. A happy-looking man in his thirties, with brown hair, rosy cheeks, and a small mustache, which he probably grew to look older. He was wearing a leather vest and chewing on a pipe stem. The smell of tobacco was strong.

Zach entered, and the man turned in his chair.

"I'm Sheriff Jed Long. Can I do somethin' for you?"

Name s Zachariah. Always figure a lawman knows what's goin' on, and 1 might be lookin' for a job. Know of any?"

They shook hands, and the lawman nodded to the stove.

Sure, but here, sit down and have some coffee."

Jed stood up and went to the small stove and shelves, finding two well-stained cups and pouring thick black liquid into them. He set them on the table and settled down on a chair next to it, crossing one leg over a knee.

Zach studied the man, wanting to trust him.

"That was a handsome woman just left," Zach said. "Emily Lassiter, a widow since her man was lynched about six months ago. Every man in town's been waitin' for her to stop wearin' black. Includin' the Scofield boys, Luke and Leroy."

"And you?"

"She wouldn't be interested in the likes of me. Bein' sheriff just makes for a short life."

"You know of any jobs?"

"It's spring, and there'll be need for roundups all over. But I just lost my deputy. He got married, and his wife made him quit. You ever wear a badge?"

"Yeah, I have. Wichita. Tucson. Couple places in Wyoming and Montana territories."

"So what's your full name?"

"Zach Lassiter."

The sheriff looked up slowly with new respect. "The town tamer? Ricky told me about you. You're his brother."

"So you know why I'm here."

Jed Long leaned back in his chair with a shrug. Zach felt his eyes burning, his stomach turning hard, waiting for the lawman to tell him who the killers were. But the answer left Zach all the more frustrated.

"Never found out who done it. Everyone knows it was a mistake. Ricky weren't no rustler."

"Does his wife know anything about it?"

"She says she was home, waitin' supper until after midnight, but she don't know I went to their house that night about nine, 'counta Ricky was to have a shotgun fixed up for me. But the lamps were turned down mighty low, and no one answered the door, and I banged pretty loud for nigh on ten minutes."

Zach was startled and lowered his cup. He tried to appear unaffected, but his mind was churning. Emily had lied? That was unthinkable. His hand was unsteady on his cup, and his mouth was dry as he spoke.

"So where was she?"

"Don't know. But it's for sure she didn't hang him. And no use startin' any gossip. You know how folks are. So you keep that bit of news to yourself."

Zach sipped his coffee, words failing him.

"Now, I know you're here fixin' to find out who killed Ricky, but I can tell you this. You go stirrin' up trouble, you'll make the guilty mighty nervous, and they'll be bound to stop you, one way or another."

"I figure if I make 'em nervous. I'll learn a thing or two."

"Could be you're right."

"I ran into Oscar Wallace on the trail. And Sally Scofield. They offered me a job."

She's been out here about a year. Everyone figures she's gonna marry the bank manager, Simon Oliver, a fancy educated man who showed up a couple months after she got here."

"Tell me about Scofield."

"Levi's got the biggest spread this part of the state, and rustlers been hittin' him hard. He's hired some rough-looking hombres. The meanest is Red Primo."

"Primo?"

"Gunman looking for a reputation. He'll be after yours, you can bet on it. Anyhow, I ain't never been able to find out nothin' from anyone out there. They got a pretty tight lip."

Zach grinned. "Sally Scofield didn't seem one bit short of words."

Jed relit his pipe and puffed on it. "Don't be gettin' ideas about her. Levi would blow a hole in you. She grew up in Missouri with his sister, 'counta his wife died when she was born, but there was some trouble they ain't talkin' about, and she moved out here."

Zach sobered and leaned back, his big hands playing with the coffee cup. "Tell me about Ricky."

"Well, it happened about thirty miles east of town at Coyote Creek, right where the Scofield spread ends and you run into the Square T, run by Ray Tealman. That's where Ricky was delivering a rifle. They claim he was there and long gone afore ten o'clock that night. But I keep wonderin' if maybe Ricky saw somethin' they was hiding, and maybe they followed 'im and strung him up. But I ain't got no proof."

"Maybe I'll find out for myself."

"You're a lawman by trade and I could use a hand. I got a deputy badge in the drawer over there, just waitin'. How about it? You'd be able to ask all the questions you want."

Zach was thoughtful; then he nodded.

Quickly, the lawman went to his desk and pulled out a badge, ready to swear in Zach before he changed his mind.

"All right," Zach said. "I'll take it, but I won't be showin' it tonight. I wanta hear what the town's got to say when the law ain't around."

"Now listen, you watch yourself out there. I'm hopin' hard cases like Primo will be mindin' their manners with Zach Lassiter wearin' a badge."

Zach wasn't so sure about that, and neither was Red Primo, who was back at the Scofield bunkhouse when Oscar Wallace was telling how he had run into Zach.

There were four older hands getting dandied up and splashing on toilet water. The bunkhouse was some sixty feet long and could sleep forty men. Gear and tack lay around and was hung on the walls. The room smelled of leather and sweat.

Primo had been tying a new string tie to go with his fancy new shirt. He was sitting on his bunk, his small dark eyes widening. He had a thin face, ruddy skin, and a wide mouth, and wore conchos on his gun belt and hatband. His six-gun had a pearl handle, and he claimed to have killed many a man.

Primo smiled. "Well, so Lassiter's come to town."

"Not sure he's stickin' around," Oscar Wallace said.

"He's the gunsmith's brother," a man said. "Got a big reputation. He'll be makin' trouble."

"Not with Jed Long around," another remarked.

Primo sneered. "Long can't take Lassiter."

No one dared ask Primo if he could take the gunfighter, because all of them gave Primo a wide berth, except for three young hands who saw him as some kind of hero.

Oscar Wallace pulled on his hat and walked outside, wondering how long it would take for Primo to go after Lassiter, a man he had liked at first meeting.

He glanced at the three waddies waiting on Primo, their horses and Primo's saddled and waiting. He knew that Levi had a necessity for gunmen, but he didn't like it much. He ignored them and walked past.

The corral was filled with new mustangs they had bought in Mesilla, and every one of them was green. Oscar leaned on the fence watching them with the pleasure an old hand felt at the beginning of a new remuda.

"Hey, Oscar, you sleepin' over there?"

He turned slowly. It was Leroy Scofield, the younger brother, the one who had a lot of trouble being serious. A man who was often downright silly.

Oscar liked Leroy, who was sporting a new shirt and vest, and strutting as usual. He was twenty-five, with soft brown eyes and a handsome boyish face like his brother, but he also had a scar on his left cheek from a knife fight. He was slight of build but well muscled, and full of foolishness.

Leroy leaned on the fence next to the foreman.

"Hey, what about that skinny mare for Sally? I'll break it myself. She sure can ride. I figured with her growin' up in Missouri, she didn't know nothin'. But she can even shoot like a man. She's too good for that prissy Simon Oliver."

"Levi hear that from you?"

"Naw, Pa says she looks exactly the way Ma did when he married her, and he'll do just about anything Sally wants."

"And she wants Simon Oliver?"

"Hey, Oscar, you know what any woman's thinkin'?"

Oscar grinned. "Nope."

"You goin' into town with us? I got to see this Zach Lassiter. Maybe I'll push him around a little."

"You ain't no gun hand."

Leroy chuckled. "I've been practicin'. Besides, ain't nobody ever talks back to a Scofield."

"This Lassiter ain't got no idea how important you are."

The youth had to laugh. "Come on, Oscar. You never take me serious. Hey, don't forget the big dance cornin' up a month from Friday. I'm a real high stepper, and you can bet on it."

Later that day, men began to gather in Reata. Sundown brought red sky and a chill. Riders came from all directions. Some were strangers looking a bit shady, others just saddle tramps riding the grub line.

Most of the hands had crowded into the Lucky Lady Saloon, a smoky, crowded establishment with a walnut bar and a roulette wheel. There were no women, but it was popular because of the wiry piano player, who played a lively tune and sang like a frog. Tonight was no exception, with "The Girl I Left Behind Me" and his rocky voice filling the room.

> *"I'm lonesome since I crossed the hill,*
> *And o'er the moor and valley;*
> *Such heavy thoughts my heart do fill,*
> *Since parting with my Sally—"*

The lilting tune caught Zach's attention. He was in a poker game at a corner table when Oscar saw him, and the foreman walked over to pull up a chair. The other three men were merchants in shirtsleeves, chewing on cigars as they studied their cards. One was skinny and two were very fat. There was an empty bottle on the table and empty glasses in front of the merchants, with no glass in front of Zach.

Zach's deputy badge was under his vest, pinned to his shirt and out of sight, as he wanted to see what he could find out before anyone knew he was with the law. He had told the merchants his first name only.

"Buy you a drink?" Oscar offered.

Zach shook his head. "No, thanks. Want to sit in?"

"I just wanted to warn you about Red Primo." The foreman pulled up a chair, but didn't deal himself into the game.

"I heard."

"Don't let him push you into a gunfight."

"I ain't lookin' for one."

The skinny merchant grunted. "Stranger, maybe you could do the town a favor and get rid of Primo."

"I heard that."

The voice was sharp, arrogant, and the merchant began to sweat. Primo was there, coming out of the crowd to stand near the table.

Zach looked up to see the ruddy-faced man, who wasn't very tall but had a solid frame, his silver conchos gleaming in the lamplight. Primo was arrogant and smiling, with a sinister glow in his eyes. His voice was mocking, challenging.

"So you're Zach Lassiter."

The startled merchants stared from Zach to the gunman, and

they folded their cards, getting up and excusing themselves in a hurry. Other men turned to watch with dismay. Oscar Wallace stood up and glared at Primo.

"Go on your way, Red. We got a game goin' here."

"I just want to see what a reputation looks like."

Zach was sitting straight in his chair, annoyed that the game was broken up and not wanting to get involved with this cocky young rooster.

"Hey, Lassiter, you chicken?" Primo mocked. Slowly, Zach stood up and pushed his hat back from his brow with his left hand, his voice irritated.

"You got a problem?"

Primo grinned. "I ain't never killed me a fancy man before."

THREE

*Z*ach stood behind the table, his right hand hooked in his gun belt near his low-slung holster. Smoke and the smell of whiskey hung in the air. There was a long, breathless silence.

Zach spoke quietly, but his voice was edged with ice. "I got no business with you."

"You got a big name, Lassiter, but I can take you easy," Primo said.

"I got no time for you."

Primo was getting anxious, his hands near his six-guns, his small eyes gleaming like hot coals. His thin face was reddening, and his wide mouth was twisted into a sneer.

Zach knew the man was going to draw. He felt sweat trickling down his back. He was tight all over, but his hand was ready. Yet he was in no hurry to kill a man, and he was sick of gunfights.

Primo's mouth twitched. It was now.

But before Primo could move, Zach's six-gun snapped into his hand. Primo's mouth fell open, and his hand hung shaking at the six-gun still in his holster.

Everyone stared. Zach held the Colt steady, aimed at the gunman's gut.

No one had seen Zach draw. Oscar Wallace was so amazed that he was speechless. The crowd was hushed, everyone waiting to see if Zach was going to pull the trigger. Zach's voice was deep with anger and annoyance.

"I was enjoyin' me a game of poker, and I figure you oughta be on your way."

Primo was shamed, embarrassed, his eyes burning, but he smiled as if he were accepting the situation. He tipped his hat back, trying to be nonchalant even as his face got redder by the moment. His voice was forced.

"Sure, Lassiter. I was just funnin'."

Zach slowly holstered his six-gun and everyone relaxed. There was some nervous laughter. Zach stood quiet behind the table, waiting. Primo's face was dark red as he turned his back and started toward the entrance.

Suddenly Primo spun, six-gun in hand.

Zach was already lifting the empty bottle and hurling it like a cannonball. The bottle struck Primo square in the gut, and he heaved, gasping for air, his gun nearly slipping from his grasp. He had lost his edge, and he doubled up, fury gripping him. He started to raise his weapon just as Jed's voice rang out.

"Primo, back off."

Primo hesitated. He looked to the side to see the sheriff standing there with a shotgun aimed at him. The gunman still paused, but when he saw the steady gleam in Jed Long's gaze, he knew he'd better stop. "All right, sheriff. We was just havin' fun." Primo slowly holstered his weapon, but he was still having trouble breathing. He turned to leave with several of his friends, but he paused by the swinging doors to look back, his snarl fierce with yellow teeth showing. "We ain't finished, Lassiter."

Then he was gone. Zach felt relief surging through him, and he nodded to Jed Long, who went outside to be sure that Primo was leaving. But Zach could barely sit on his chair, tension still holding him numb. Oscar Wallace wiped his brow. "Whew."

A cowhand picked up the bottle from the floor, proclaiming it as a souvenir. Laughter eased the tension.

The noise returned to the saloon, and the piano player started up with "Sweet Betsy from Pike." The merchants cautiously gathered their chips and left for the night, and Oscar sat alone with Zach.

But a good-looking, stocky man with a small brown mustache and searching dark eyes came over to them. He looked like a rancher, his hat worn and soiled, his bandanna sagging. He reached out his hand to Zach, who noticed the man was also right-handed. Zach carefully shook his hand.

"Ray Tealman. I just saw your action there, Mr. Lassiter, and I could use a man like you."

Zach considered this as he leaned back. Tealman's had been where Ricky had delivered the rifle the night he died. And the sheriff suspected Ricky might have seen something at the Square T that had put his life on the line. Zach studied the rancher, then shrugged.

"Thanks. I'll have to think on it."

"Well, job's open."

"I heard my brother was lynched on your place."

Tealman grunted. "Not exactly. They got him along Coyote Creek, which borders it."

"Know who done it?"

"No. And I figure you oughta let the law handle it."

"I am the law."

Zach lifted his vest to reveal the deputy's badge pinned to his shirt. Tealman's eyes narrowed. Bystanders stared, as did Oscar. After a moment, the rancher recovered.

"Well, then, let me know if I can help you any. My boys, they don't know nothin' about any lynchin', but they'd be right happy to show you around."

The man shuffled off into the noisy crowd. Zach gazed after him, wondering. Tealman had become defensive. After a moment, Zach decided to pin his badge on his vest, with everyone staring.

Oscar was thoughtful, studying Zach, who avoided his gaze. Then the foreman shrugged. "Ray's all right. But I see you already got yourself a job. Ricky always said you was a natural-born lawman."

"Maybe so."

"But right now, looks like everyone's afraid to get in your game."

"I'll sit in."

Oscar looked up, then hurried to his feet. "Levi."

Zach leaned back for a look at this royal rancher. The man was solid with tough features, his eyes gray but friendly, and his rather large nose reaching down to a heavy handlebar mustache of graying brown hair. He was wearing a leather coat and a weathered old Stetson.

"You been here all along?" Oscar asked.

"Sure have. Was over in that far corner, but I seen everything. I'd like to talk to Mr. Lassiter here."

Zach nodded, and the rancher pulled up a chair.

"I'm Levi Scofield. And I like what I saw. You handled that rooster Primo just right. First you outdrew and shamed him, and then you gutted him with a bottle when he tried to sneak a shot at you."

"Primo ain't gonna let things ride," Oscar said.

Zach shrugged his big shoulders and shuffled the cards.

Levi leaned forward. "What I saw told me plenty about you, Zach. You coulda killed Primo, but you didn't. You got no brag in you. I like that about a man. Shows restraint. And it means in a real fight, you'd keep your head. And you won't be killin' for the fun of it."

Oscar was uncomfortable. "Maybe I'd better leave."

"No," the rancher said. "You and my sons are the only ones know what 1 got to say. And Zach, I'd sure like you to come to work for me. We got plenty of trouble, and I need a man like you."

Zach was uneasy. "Thanks, Mr. Scofield, but I have a job."

"Jed Long would understand. And you could name your price."

"It ain't no secret Ricky Lassiter was my brother, and that's why I'm here. And I figure a badge is gonna help me find out what happened."

Levi studied Zach for a long moment. He made a face, was thoughtful, then shrugged and leaned back in his chair, clearing his throat.

"All right, then I got no choice. You and Jed Long, you both got to know my business. Mind if we walk over and see 'im afore he turns in?"

Zach was curious. Maybe Levi knew something Zach wanted to know, something about the lynching. He stood up

23

and walked out with him and Oscar. The night air was cold and crisp. Levi led the way across to the sheriff's office, where a light was burning.

Jed Long greeted them with his blackened cups and strong coffee, and the four men sat about the table with Levi Scofield bursting to say his piece.

"Boys," the rancher said, "I got me thirty hands out at the ranch right now, and a half dozen of them can use a gun pretty fancy. But they ain't enough." Zach sipped his coffee. "Enough for what?"

"To protect Sally."

Surprised, Zach and Jed Long glanced at each other. The sheriff spoke first. "Protect her from what?" Oscar Wallace watched the street from the window. Levi was wound up pretty tight, and it was obvious he had a bellyful to spill.

Levi cleared his throat. "Ain't had no reason to tell you this, Jed, until now, and I don't want it goin' no further than this room. Now, Sally lived most of her life in Missouri. My sister took her when my wife died at childbirth. And Sally grew up to be a real lady. All the fellas were courtin' her from the time she was sixteen, but my sister kept a tight rein."

Zach was getting mighty curious. "And?"

"Sally never got real interested until this schoolteacher came along when she was eighteen, about four years ago. Fellow called Fletcher Dannack, an educated man, a fancy talker. She was real impressed. So was my sister, who wrote me about this fine man who was perfect for Sally."

Zach pushed his hat back. "And?"

"Well, the way it came out, about three years ago ole Fletcher went off to St. Joseph on some business, and he was recognized and arrested. Seems he'd killed a man in a bank robbery a couple of years before, in Kansas. Turned out Dannack was a dangerous man named Fletcher Hickman, who'd killed a lot of men up in Wyoming in gunfights. They claim he even rode with the James boys but left 'em before they headed for Northfield."

Jed nodded. "I heard about Hickman, all right." There was a long pause while Levi rearranged his bandanna, as if it was choking him. He looked tired, and his voice was getting deeper.

"Sally near fell apart when she found out the truth. She was already working on her wedding dress. But in 'seventy-seven, Fletcher Hickman was sent up for twenty years. Then my sister died, a year ago, and we brung Sally out here."

The rancher drew a deep breath, then continued. "Well, sir, Hickman had some fancy relatives back East, and some politicians got involved. Seems they was saying how he was so well-educated and couldn't have done all that was said at the trial, and the witness who identified him, well, that feller changed his mind all of a sudden. Six weeks ago, Fletcher Hickman got himself a pardon and got the court to change his name to Dannack to hide his reputation. And I'm figurin' he'll be headed this way, lookin' for Sally."

Jed shrugged. "He ain't going to do anything that'll send him back to prison."

"He's a free man," Levi said, "but he's dangerous. And since he's a fast gun, the best I figured I could do was hire ourselves one that's maybe a little faster. And Zach, from what I saw in the saloon, you're plenty fast. Could be, you're the fastest there is."

Jed Long sipped his coffee. "You offered Zach a job?"

"He turned me down," Levi said. "But to get on with it, now

Sally, she don't know Fletcher got hisself free, and I ain't gonna tell her, 'counta I could be wrong. He may never show up."

"You think she wants to see him now?" Zach asked.

"Well, son, I ain't never been able to figure out any female. But Sally, she's likely the most fetchin' woman a man can find west of the Mississippi. And I hear this man was right crazy about her. Wore her on his arm like some kind of decoration."

Zach was thoughtful. Under other circumstances, he would protect a woman like Sally for free.

"Name your price, Zach," Levi persisted. "She's my only daughter."

"Your decision, Zach," the sheriff told him.

But Zach didn't want his hands tied. "Sorry, Mr. Scofield. You got to understand. I'm here to find out who killed my brother. But I'll help all I can."

"All right. But why don't you ride out with us in the morning anyway? Take a look at our spread. Spend a couple nights. Wearin' that badge, you'll be huntin' rustlers anyhow, and we've sure had our share of trouble with 'em. About ten months ago, they started pickin' us off."

The sheriff nodded. "Good idea, Zach. I ain't had much time to look around out there."

"Now, you don't tell nobody Dannack's coming,"

Levi said. "And that includes Sally. She'll find out soon enough if he shows."

Zach stood up, shaking the rancher's hand, finding his grip strong. It wouldn't be hard to like this man.

Oscar Wallace put his hand on Zach's shoulder.

"Glad you're ridin' out with us, Zach. And don't worry too much about Primo. I'll try to keep him on a short rope."

"See you at sunup at the livery," Levi said. "You stayin' at the hotel same as us?"

"I have to call on Ricky's widow, but I'll walk part way with you."

The three men left Jed and went outside. They strolled from the shadows to the light of a lantern hung in front of a store. They paused as a man appeared on the boardwalk up the street, heading their way. He was walking toward them, holding a cane. Dressed in a fine black coat and wearing a small-brimmed hat, his collar white and fixed, the man looked like a politician.

"Here comes Simon Oliver," Levi murmured. "He got here a couple of months after Sally came. Runs the bank right well, and he's been courtin' her. But he ain't to know about Fletcher Dannack."

Simon came up to them, the moonlight pale on his handsome, long face. A man like this would impress a woman. He had an air of importance, yet his smile was broad and friendly. He twirled his cane and greeted them.

"Mr. Scofield. Isn't it a grand evening?"

Levi introduced Zach as the new deputy and Ricky's brother, and the man was startled.

"Well, Reata has room for everyone, Mr. Lassiter. Ricky talked about you often."

They spoke casually for a few minutes, and then the banker was on his way down the street. Levi turned to gaze after him.

"Simon works nights, days, weekends, all the time. I guess he wants to be somebody and have a lot of money someday. And everyone likes the man."

"Yeah," Oscar said, "but he's a little too perfect."

"Oscar thinks Sally's his daughter," Levi said with a grin.

Zach swallowed, thinking of Sally. Well, she wasn't for him anyhow. And he already had a girl on his mind. But he didn't much like Simon Oliver. Oscar was right. The man was too perfect, and that was always suspect.

At the hotel, Zach said good night and headed up the alley.

It was getting late, but he knew he had to see Emily before he left. He found his way to the back street behind the hotel and located the boardinghouse. Lights were still burning in the parlor.

He knocked on the door several times.

At length, a small woman opened the door. She was maybe fifty, and charming, with a big smile, a button nose, and spectacles; she wore a full apron over her gray dress. He had expected an elderly lady and was surprised, his hand still suspended in the air.

"Well, young man, did you hurt your hand?"

"No, ma'am."

"I'm Ma Rindell. But I got no rooms."

"Sorry, ma'am. I need to see Mrs. Lassiter."

She glanced at his badge, then allowed him to enter the well-lighted hallway. She led him to the plush parlor, where Emily was seated in a soft chair, a large book in her hands. She lowered the book and straightened, surprised. Wearing black, she still looked wonderful. Her blond hair was drawn back, and her eyes were shining.

Ma Rindell left them alone, and Zach pulled up a chair close to Emily and sat down, his voice low as he greeted her and removed his hat. But all the while, he was wondering why she had lied to the sheriff. Yet her grief was obvious, and he didn't want to upset her with accusations.

She was staring at his badge.

"Emily, I just wanted to tell you I'm workin' for Jed. Maybe wearin' a badge will help me find out what I want to know."

She was startled, her voice a whisper. "But if Jed Long didn't find out who murdered Ricky, how can you?"

"I don't figure anything happens without Scofield's say-so. I'll be spendin' some time out there, see what I can learn."

She looked weary and sad. "After what happened to Ricky, I've been so depressed. And part of it is this black dress. I'm ready to stop mourning. It'll never bring Ricky back, and I can't bear the loneliness."

"Ricky would want you to go on. Now if you need me, you just holler."

"All right, Zachariah."

She glanced toward the entrance to the parlor, watching for Ma Rindell, and then slid her soft fingers onto his rough hand. Her smile was affectionate.

He was overwhelmed and was about to rise, but she slid her hand up his arm and pulled his shoulder forward. She leaned toward him, and to his dismay, she pressed her lips to his, then drew back slowly.

"I always cared for you, Zachariah."

Swallowing so hard it hurt, he stared at her as she drew back, and then stumbled to his feet, pulling his hat on, nodding and backing away from her sweet smile.

As he entered the hallway, he could see through the dining room to the faraway kitchen, where Ma Rindell was rolling dough with her back to him.

Outside, he drew a deep breath. His heart was crazy in his chest. Five years, and she was still affectionate, still cared for him. Yet he felt nothing.

He headed back to the hotel, while Emily folded her book and glanced at the big mahogany grandfather's clock near the back wall. She stood up slowly, smoothing her dress.

Emily headed up the stairs, a little out of breath, her face warm. She had always liked Zach, but he had not been a good prospect. Wearing a badge, he could have been shot anytime. No, Ricky had been her best choice, even though she had lost him under painful circumstances.

And Zach had turned into a gunfighter, a roamer.

Reaching the landing, she looked back at the soft glow of the lamps in the empty parlor. The two elderly male boarders were out playing cards somewhere. The elderly lady was visiting at a friend's ranch.

A lamp hung near her door, which she unlocked, entering the room. Another lamp burned low on the dressing table. Lace decorated the curtains and bed cover. It was a small but pleasant room, with a big window.

Emily wanted a lot more than this, and she knew how to get it, no matter how long it took.

She walked to the lamp and turned up the light. Then she paused to gaze at her reflection in the mirror.

A rock pinged on her window. She hurried to lift the shade, and covered her eyes to peer outside. Looking down, she could see a man waiting for her, his hand lifted in a signal.

Quickly, she smiled and waved back, seized her shawl, and hurried to the door. She opened it a crack to carefully peer down the stairs.

FOUR

$\mathcal{U}$naware of Emily's visitor at the boardinghouse that night, Zach was lying on his hotel bed, trying to sort out his thoughts. He stared at a little spider on the ceiling, patiently making its web and trying to get over to the window.

Patience, that's what he needed. Somehow, the men who hanged Ricky were going to pay, but what was he to do about Emily? Her kiss had startled him down to his boots, but why didn't he kiss her back? What was wrong with him? All these years, he had loved her. Now he wondered if he felt anything at all. And why had she lied?

He thought of Simon Oliver. He was probably right for Sally, but why did Zach feel so annoyed?

He slept fitfully, and in the morning, his badge gleaming on his vest, he rode north with Oscar Wallace and Levi Scofield, with the sunrise red and yellow in the east. It was still cold, and an icy wind was rising. In the far north, the sky was dark.

"Storm coming," Levi said. "But I knowed it yesterday. Could feel it in my bones."

"Had a paint like that," Zach remarked.

Levi grunted, then grinned. "That a fact?" "Soon's the weather was gonna change, he got all out of sorts. Always raised a ruckus a day ahead. Even threw me on the campfire one mornin'. Sure made me mad."

"So what'd you do with 'im?"

"Shot 'im."

Levi glared at him, but Zach laughed, shaking his head.

Oscar Wallace grinned. The three men took to joking and making fun of one thing or another. Zach found himself liking Levi a little too much, and he prayed the rancher had nothing to do with Ricky's death.

"Sure is a lot of grass out here," Zach said, gazing around at the rolling hills and drifting herds.

"Gettin' crowded," Levi replied. "Everyone's after a cut of my spread. But I took this land and I earned it. For every bloody fight with the Mescalero, for every rustler and nester, my blood is scattered all over this land."

"I reckon your sons will be taking over someday." Levi nodded. "Yeah, I made 'em full partners. Trouble is, they still got a lot of foolishness in their heads, especially Leroy. But Luke, he's past thirty now, and I'm hopin' he'll settle down and make it easier on me."

"What about Sally? Will you make her a partner?" Levi grunted. "Depends who she marries. I don't want some fool cornin' on here with any rights because they got hitched. I want to see who he is. But yeah, 1 know about all that noise them women are makin' back East about bein' equal. And I know they gave 'em the vote up in Wyomin'."

"And you don't agree?" Zach persisted.

"Zach, women are already in charge of us men, and if we

give 'em any more, we'll be in real trouble."

Zach had to laugh. He sure liked this rancher.

They could see the red buttes now, marking the way. The treeless land spread in all directions, rolling with waving grass dotted with sage and palo verde.

Zach was impressed with the spread. There were many corrals with horses, several sheds and barns, a cookhouse behind a long bunkhouse, and a very pretty white, two-story house sitting on a rise of the land just beyond. Aspens had been planted around the house, the only trees in sight. A big creek cut through the land behind the house.

Leroy was waiting on the porch, staring as the men left their horses at the corral. Oscar stayed behind, and Levi headed for the house, Zach trailing. Levi reached the porch first, as his son was still staring at Zach and his badge.

"Son, this here's Zach Lassiter, Jed's new deputy. He's cornin' to help us look for rustlers. And to be on the lookout for snakes."

"The boys have been talkin' about you," Leroy said to Zach. "Sorry about your brother."

Zach nodded, grateful for the youth's obvious concern.

The house was well-furnished but simple. There were hides on the walls and floors. Nothing fancy except the big, long couch and a couple of chairs, along with blue velvet drapes. There was a big stone hearth in the living room, and a few paintings hung on the wall.

On the stairway that spiraled upward near the living room entrance, they saw Luke coming down, still buttoning his shirt. He looked sleepy and unfriendly, but he had the same boyish face as Leroy, except for the bump on his nose.

Levi introduced Zach, then led them into the big room where

the table could hold a meal for a lot of men. Leroy poured the coffee while Levi looked around.

"Where's Sally?"

"Out back at the cellar," Leroy said.

The men sat around the table, and Levi said he was still hoping Zach would take the job and help protect Sally in case Fletcher Dannack showed.

Luke frowned. "We don't need Lassiter. We'll take care of Sally ourselves."

"You got a ranch to run."

"You don't even know if Fletcher's cornin' here," Luke argued. "And if he's got a pardon, maybe he'll be behavin' hisself to stay out of trouble. Besides, Sally may not even want him around."

"You may be right," Levi agreed. "But from what I hear, he's a devious and dangerous man. He may not wait for her invitation. But even if he don't show up, we've been havin' trouble with rustlers, and I worry about Sally always ridin' alone. She just don't listen. And you never know when some Mescalero is gonna break from the reservation. We're right on the trail to Mexico."

Leroy frowned. "So what are you suggestin'?"

"Well, son," Levi said, "I'm gonna keep hopin' Zach will hang up that badge and come to work for us. He's got the experience. And I saw him in action. Not only did he outdraw Primo, but when Primo tried to pull a fast one, Zach belted him in the gut with a bottle."

"Boy," Leroy said with a grin, "wish I'd seen that."

Luke leaned back to sip his coffee. "If Sally was to marry that Simon Oliver, he might take her a long way from here."

Zach shook his head. "If Dannack's the way he sounds, no husband's going to stop 'im."

"So now what?" Luke asked his father.

"Well, Zach can have breakfast with us, and then he'll take a look around the spread. He may be stayin' a night or two."

"What about Primo?" Leroy asked, grinning.

"Well," Levi said, "Primo will be on the prod all right, but he'll behave hisself around the men. Besides, Zach's wearin' a badge. It may keep him at bay."

"I tell you, Pa," Luke said, "I don't like havin' this gunfighter around, even if he is totin' a badge."

"Ah, Luke," Leroy said with a grin. "He won't hurt you."

Luke glared at his younger brother.

They fell silent as they heard the back door open. Sally, wearing an apron over her white blouse and riding skirt, was carrying several potatoes and a chunk of wood. Her hair was in some disarray, with a shiny red lock dangling down her forehead. There was flour on her cheek. She looked mighty fetching as she smiled at Zach.

"Well, Mr. Lassiter. Fancy seeing you here."

"Zach is going to help us with them rustlers," Levi said.

She stared at Zach's badge, then smiled. "Well, Mr. Lassiter, you're certainly full of surprises. What's next?"

Zach grinned at her. "You'll figure it out."

Levi looked from Sally to Zach and back again, his face set with new curiosity. The flirting was obvious. His expression didn't reflect either approval or disapproval.

Sally gave a soft laugh and went on into the kitchen. The men talked about the rustlers while she prepared breakfast. Levi suspected some of the small ranchers, but hadn't been able to prove anything.

"I know a few Mescalero cornin' through get one now and then," Levi said, "and I don't mind a hungry Apache helpin' hisself. After all, we sorta stole their country out from under 'em, and we owe 'em somethin'. But we see a lot of shod ponies out there runnin' off strays whenever they get a chance."

Sally served them a delicious breakfast of potatoes, bacon, and eggs. She sat and ate with them, and Zach couldn't get enough of anything. He leaned back with a full belly and felt very good.

"It's sure a pretty day out," she said.

"And you ain't foolin' me," Levi added. "You got your ridin' clothes on, and I already said no more ridin' alone. But Zach wants to see the spread. Maybe he'd let you show him around."

She smiled. "But he will never be able to keep up with me, and he might get lost out there."

Zach grinned, enjoying her twinkling eyes.

"I'll go along," Leroy said.

Levi shook his head. "You and Luke ain't got them cattle counted over on the west range. No, if Zach's gonna be deputy sheriff, he's got to have a look out there."

Conversation became easier and lighter. Luke cast more than one unfriendly glance at Zach, even while others were laughing at Leroy's funny stories.

"There was this fellow named Abernathy," Leroy was saying. "He figured he'd make a lot of money ridin' trains and robbin' folks, then jumpin' off. But this one time, he was gettin' mighty friendly with this big round female with a fat purse, and she was gettin' ideas about him. They was outside back of the train, and he pulled his pistol. She was so put out, she picked him right up and throwed him off the train. Poor Abernathy landed on his head. He still thinks he's married to her and goes wanderin' around, lookin' for her." Everyone laughed, but Levi grunted.

"Trains are ruinin' the West. By next year, the SP's gonna join up with the Santa Fe down in Deming. Then there's gonna be a lot more farmers movin' in and crowdin' us."

"The railroads have their own problems," Zach remarked. "Like trying to have a time schedule across the country. They're talking about changing everybody's clocks as they cross the country so's folks would be on different times when the train gets there." Leroy laughed. "Why, that's plumb silly. You mean they'd want Reata to have a different time than them folks in New York? Now I know them railroaders are loco. How they gonna know what time they're gettin' anywheres?"

"By then," Zach said, "there may be telephones all the way out here. They can call to find out."

Levi grunted. "Them things will never work. Besides, who needs 'em? All you have to do is stick your head out a window and holler. That's just as good." Luke, who had been simmering, straightened in his chair. "Well, Pa, me and Leroy better head out."

"Now then," Levi said to Luke. "You got a bun under your saddle over Zach here. Mind tellin' me why?"

"I don't trust 'im, that's all."

Luke grunted and stalked out of the room.

Levi watched his sons leave, Sally walking outside with them, and he turned to Zach. "I figure Luke's got a yen for Emily Lassiter, and if he figured you was gonna go callin', he'd be plenty jealous. Luke's not taken to any woman much over the years, but after Emily's husband was killed, he started lookin' after her."

"I'm not courtin' her."

"Whatever you do, Zach, I'm sure it'll be the honorable thing."

Zach was grateful for the man's trust, and he found that riding with Sally was fun. She rode like a Comanche and never tired. Her smile was always ready, and her laugh was like music. As they rode, he thought of Emily, and his thoughts were ever more confused.

But there was no denying that Sally was gorgeous. He liked seeing her crimson hair blowing around her and shining in the hot sun. Her dark green eyes were bright and interested in everything.

She liked to race, and he let her win. Reining up, she laughed. "Where did you learn to ride, Mr. Lassiter?"

"On a donkey, I reckon."

Giggling, she rode on ahead, and he watched her with delight. She was so different from Emily. He didn't know how to feel, but he was sure enjoying himself.

As they later rode side by side, she turned to him. "Can you hit anything with that six-shooter?"

He grinned. "I'm just waiting for that match we're gonna have. What are the stakes?"

"Five dollars?"

"If you win, all right. But me, I get to name my prize."

"No, Mr. Lassiter, I don't trust you."

"Now that's a fine thing to say to a gentleman riding with you in the middle of nowhere."

She smiled. "You wouldn't be here if Levi didn't trust you, so I suppose I'll have to."

"Good. I'll let you know the prize after I win."

"Oh, no. Before the match starts, you have to say it."

He grinned, and they set their mounts into a gallop. By late afternoon, they were up on a rise looking down several hundred feet into a canyon with red walls and a trickling creek.

"We call it Apache Canyon," she said.

They dismounted there to rest their horses in the shade of some boulders. They loosened the cinches, then sat near each other on the grass, leaning on the rocks. Shadows were long, and they knew it would be dark before they returned home, but neither was in a hurry.

"I heard about your brother. I'm sorry."

He nodded his thanks and looked away.

"Are you married, Mr. Lassiter?"

"Nope."

"Ever want to be?"

"A long time ago."

"What happened?"

"She married someone else."

Sally smiled gently. "Do you consider yourself lucky?"

"I ain't figured that out yet. What about you and this Simon Oliver? You gonna marry him?"

"He's a nice man. He'll be coming to supper, and you can meet him."

He leaned back. "You didn't answer my question."

"And you didn't answer mine."

Zach grinned, pushing his hat back. He felt lazy and sleepy. Sitting here with Sally Scofield as twilight neared, with passing clouds to read and a breeze rising, it was mighty pleasant.

But there were things he had to know.

"You ever hear any talk about who might have murdered my brother?"

"No, I'm sorry. But everyone thinks it was a mistake. Your brother was no rustler. And there are a lot of new faces both here and at Tealman's. Any of them could have done it."

They fell silent, watching the colors change across the land. After a while, she turned to him slowly and sadly.

"I guess you've known a lot of outlaws, Zach?"

"Sure."

"Were they bad men?"

"Some are still fighting the War between the States. A lot of 'em are still good men but they got lost. Others, well, they took the easy way out from workin'. And them's the ones to look out for."

"I knew one. Back in Missouri. He was teaching school. The children loved him. He was a wonderful dancer, and he asked me to marry him. I was overwhelmed by his charm. But one day we heard he was arrested in St. Joseph for murder and robbery. He's in prison now."

"And how did you feel about that?"

"I lost faith in myself and in my judgment. I had been so sure of everything. I was making my wedding dress. There was going to be a big dance for us. And then suddenly, the man I knew was gone. How could I have been so wrong and so serious about a man who was really a killer?"

"I read once where every man is three men. The one folks think he is, the one he fancies he is, and the man he really is."

"And which man are you?"

He shrugged. "Well, I reckon folks think I'm a gunfighter. Me, I think I'm a lawman by nature, but I want my own spread someday."

"And the man you really are?"

"If I knew that, I'd sure be a lot better off. But maybe it's that fellow who lies out on the prairie at night, starin' at the stars and talkin' to the Lord."

He was suddenly embarrassed by his words, his face hot. He realized he had exposed his heart for the first time, never having admitted anything to anyone.

But he saw softness in her smile. "You sound like a lonely man, Zach Lassiter."

He looked away, staring down into the canyon, her words hanging in the air. Lonely he had been for a long time, but here with Sally, gazing across the land as twilight neared, he felt peace and comfort. Yet he couldn't dare hope she had any more interest in him than a mere flirtation.

Sally pushed her hair from her face. "I suppose that applies to women. Everyone in Missouri thinks I'm an empty-headed debutante. And here, Levi's always worrying about me for one reason or another. And Simon Oliver, the banker, he just thinks I'm some kind of china doll. They all see me differently, I guess."

"And you?"

"I think I'm a woman who would make a fine wife and mother."

"Even if you could outride and outshoot 'im?"

She laughed. "Even then."

"And the woman you really are?"

Darkness clouded her face. "I don't know. Sometimes I lie awake at night wondering. Even though I target shoot, I could never hurt anyone, not even a lizard. My aunt used to laugh at me because I'd let flies out the door instead of swatting them. And then she died, and I cried for weeks. Maybe that's what I am. Foolish and weak."

They were silent a long moment. Zach found himself liking her intensely. He knew more about this woman now than he had ever known about Emily, who was like a living portrait of a proper young woman. Sally was open, her smile both joyful and teasing, yet with honesty prevailing.

"You ain't weak," he said. "God made you a woman, that's all. You got to be strong and soft at the same time, and that ain't easy."

"And you, Zach? Did He make you a gunfighter?" "No, I did that all by myself. Most of the reputation I got came from wearin' a badge. But I reckon I ain't too proud of it."

"What are you proud of?"

He shrugged, wondering himself. "Well, I ain't never stole nothin'. My word is good. I cleaned up a couple of pretty rough towns as a lawman. Every fight I've been in was fair and square. I ain't never done anything I'm ashamed of."

"You know, Zach, my father likes you." Abruptly, Zach stood up and looked beyond the rim and down. "Some dust cornin' up the canyon."

She turned to follow his gaze to the canyon floor far below. They could see about eighty head of cattle and five riders coming from the west. As the herd neared, Sally suddenly stood up, her hand to her throat.

"Zach, look. That old brindle leader with the broken horn. He was rustled some time ago. Those are Levi's cattle. And those have got to be rustlers."

"You stay here, and don't move."

"But I have a rifle."

"Then cover me if you have to, but I don't want them to know you're here. Got that?"

She made a face. "All right."

She pulled her rifle from the scabbard and knelt on the rocks. Zach tightened the cinch and mounted his bay, then paused to gaze at her. She couldn't swat a fly but was determined to fight if necessary. Whether she could follow through, Zach was not so sure, but she'd be safe up here.

"Now stay put," he ordered.

Turning his bay, he rode north on the rim of the canyon and was soon on a downward slope. The narrow pass was about to end, and he had to get there before the herd.

He rode down a grade, his horse riding the dirt on its rear, and they got to the bottom and the canyon entrance faster than expected. He saw the rustlers' dust winding around the rock wall.

One man was in the lead, startled to see Zach there waiting, sitting straight in the saddle with his badge gleaming in the late-afternoon sun.

The point man came slowly forward. He had a mean face, narrow eyes, and a scraggly black beard. A poorly rolled cigarette dangled from his fat lips. His voice was hoarse.

"You lost, mister?"

"Not me. But you sure are, and them cattle ain't."

The man snarled, his hand sliding down his hip toward his six-gun. "I ain't never seen you before."

"You reach for that gun, and you won't see nobody ever again."

But the man grabbed for his gun, and Zach drew so fast that he was firing before the man's weapon cleared leather.

Eyes wild, the rustler gasped and jerked back, a hole in his chest. But he pulled his gun and was doubling up as he tried to aim it. Then he collapsed, and as he slid from the saddle, his gun went off.

The bullet slammed into Zach's left arm above the elbow. It threw his arm back, and blood gushed forth in a stream. The shock lasted a second, and then terrible pain shot up to his shoulder and down to his wrist, numbing his left hand. His six-gun still in hand, he pressed his thumb on the fountain of blood, trying to stem it.

When the rustler hit the dirt, the cattle bellowed and tried to get around them. One steer slammed against Zach's bay, and the horse went down on its forelegs, then jumped up and aside. Dust was nearly blinding, and Zach tried to rein to the side to avoid the cattle, as blood flowed down his left arm.

He could see the four drag riders coming fast behind the running cattle. He readied his weapon and waited. As the cattle passed, the dust cleared. The rustlers looked as mean as the dead man, their faces wild and bearded, but they were already aiming their six-guns.

Zach was in one heck of a spot. His left arm was bleeding badly and felt as if there were a knife in it. The pain was riding up to his shoulder and neck, then shooting down again.

He drew his breath and weighed his chances, with five bullets still in his six-gun and four men racing toward him at full speed.

And lead began to fly.

FIVE

Zach reined his bay to the side of the red rock canyon near the east entrance. The eighty-odd head of cattle had already passed. One rustler lay dead and trampled in the dust.

Somewhere back along the ridge, Sally Scofield was out of range with her rifle. Blood was still running down Zach's left arm, and the pain was shooting up his shoulder.

Four rustlers were racing toward Zach with six-guns drawn, while Zach had five bullets left. He fired and hit the first one dead center, but he couldn't avoid the charging horse.

The animal plowed into his, throwing the dead rustler to the side, causing the bay to crash against the canyon wall and drop to its knees. As Zach righted his mount, he fired at the oncoming rider just as a bullet slammed into his right side and caused him to miss.

Another bullet slammed into his bay's neck, and the animal reared and twisted, even as Zach fired and hit the oncoming rider square between the eyes.

As his horse fell beneath him, Zach fired at the next rider, hitting him in the chest. The man kept coming until his face turned white and he gasped, falling from the saddle.

Zach leaped aside from his fallen horse and aimed at the third rider, who was screaming with anger as he galloped toward him, waving his six-gun. Zach shot him between the eyes, and it was a long staggering moment before the man jerked and fell from the saddle.

Zach jumped aside from the charging horse and lost his footing, stumbling over his struggling mount. He dropped to one knee, seeing the last rider hanging off the saddle on the far side, Comanche style, and heading right toward him.

Zach shoved a hasty bullet into his six-gun, fired, and hit the man's shoulder. He tried to get at his rifle, but his dying horse was lying on its right side, and he couldn't budge it in time.

He spun, preparing to leap forward and seize the reins of the oncoming horse. The man suddenly reared up in the saddle and aimed at Zach.

As Zach jumped aside, a rifle barked from the rim above, and the man yelled as a bullet cut through his neck and down into his chest. The horse stumbled and fell, throwing the screeching man, then leaped up and trotted away.

Zach gasped for air, dropping to his knees. He was losing a lot of blood, dark fluid spurting from his left arm like a fountain. He holstered his gun and grabbed the wound, trying to stop the flow, but he was already fading.

It seemed forever before he looked up through a daze to see Sally riding down into the canyon. She was still carrying her rifle, and she looked shattered. Having just killed a man, she looked ill, her face devoid of color.

Sliding from the saddle, she knelt in front of Zach.

"Are you all right?" he asked, weaving.

She was shaking all over, but she grabbed his right arm to steady him. "You're bleeding fast."

"He hit the right spot, that's for sure."

"Sit down, Zach."

She pressed her fingers to the wound, and the longer she held them in place, the more the bleeding slowed. Tears were trickling down her face. Her voice was wavering.

"Hold your hand here."

She was a blur now, but he did as she ordered. She placed a small rock on the wound, then bound it with her red bandanna. It stopped the flow. She took his bandanna and tied it above the wound, tightly.

"We have to get you home, Zach."

"My horse—"

"It's hurt bad. I think it's dying."

"You'll have to shoot it."

"I can't."

"Help me, and I'll do it."

The painful chore was done with Sally holding the rifle and Zach pulling the trigger. All the while tears streamed down her face, and she was choking on them. But he was barely conscious.

"Zach, I have to get you on my horse before you faint."

He nodded, struggling to his feet with her arm about him. "The cattle, are they gone?"

"No sign of them. And their horses ran off. We'll try to pick one up, but I have to get you to the ranch."

She managed to get his boot in the stirrup, and with all his fading strength, he pulled himself into the saddle as she pushed him. Using saddle strings, she tied his wrists to the saddle horn and pommel. Then she stood on a rock and swung onto the cantle behind him, taking the reins. He was swaying, and she had trouble holding him steady.

The last thing he remembered was her arms around him.

*   *   *

It was late that night before Zach came to consciousness again in a dark room, on a bed. He was on the second floor of the ranch house. Moonlight sifted through the lace curtains on the right wall. A smoky lamp burned low on the dresser. The door was open, but he could see only the railing that led to the stairs.

He could hear Sally talking to Levi and another man in the hallway outside his door.

"Well, Miss Sally," the other man said. "You saved his life. That bullet hit an artery and he was losing blood fast. But you stopped it."

"Doc," Levi cut in, "how long you figure he'll be laid up?"

"Well, he's a strong man. I suppose it'll be a week before he has enough blood back in him, but in a day or so, he should be able to move around. Keep that arm in a sling like I showed you."

"Thanks, Doc."

"Now then, Miss Sally, you had a terrible experience today. Do you want something to help you sleep?"

"No, I'll be all right."

Zach heard footsteps going down the stairs. He felt for his six-gun, but he wasn't wearing his gun belt. At least he still had his clothes on, except for his boots. Then he saw his gun hanging in its holster on the bedpost behind him.

Zach lay quiet, his head aching and his left arm bound so tight even the bandages hurt. It was numb and in a sling.

He heard a door slam downstairs, and then he heard Sally talking to the rancher near the foot of the staircase.

"Doc was right," Levi said. "You had a bad experience. For a man to have to kill another man, that's bad enough. But for you, well, you're gonna be a long time forgettin'."

"I'm having bad dreams, and I'm still awake."

"Well, you did a brave thing, Sally. Now you go on up to bed, and I'll sit with Zach."

"No, I don't want to go to bed until I can barely keep my eyes open. I'll stay with him."

"All right. I'll spell you in a couple of hours, but it's nearly three in the mornin'."

Zach could hear footsteps coming up the stairs. Levi's heavy ones turned away on the landing. He saw a shadow in the doorway, and Sally came slowly into the dark room. The soft glow of the lamp danced in her hair. He closed his eyes. She pulled up a chair near him and slumped in it.

"Zach, are you awake?"

He didn't move, then heard her softly crying. It hurt him, and he opened his eyes to watch the way she was burying her face in her hands, trying to be quiet.

After a while, she stopped shaking. She leaned back and wiped her eyes and face with a handkerchief. She was having trouble controlling herself, but at length, she became quiet. Zach pretended sleep, allowing her privacy.

After a time, he moved as if awakening.

"Zach?"

He looked up at her. "My arm hurts like blazes."

"But it was your left arm, at least."

She leaned forward, sliding her chair to the side of the bed to be closer. Zach gazed at her in the pale light. She was incredible. He spoke with an effort.

"You're one heck of a shot, getting that rustler on the run that way."

"I'm not proud of it, Zach. I've been doing a lot of praying."

He touched his left arm. "Sure is stiff."

"Doc said not to change the bandages for twenty-four hours. You may be in bed for a week."

"Not a chance. I'll be up for breakfast."

"Well, you'll have breakfast in bed, and you'll stay in this guest room until I say you can move."

"Is that a fact?"

"Yes."

He grinned and extended his right hand, so weak he could barely lift it. She slid her soft white fingers into the fold of his rough, weathered ones, and he felt a trickle of pleasure running up his arm.

Her green eyes were so dark and lovely, her hair the color of a wild sunrise, and her smile as gentle as a child's. Zach just plain enjoyed staring at her.

"You sure got some freckles," he said.

She blushed. "When I was little, my aunt said they were angel dust that stayed."

He wanted to tease her some more, but he felt faint, and the next thing he knew, he was back in that pool of darkness.

When morning came, he awakened to the smell of bacon and eggs and hot coffee, and he realized he was mighty hungry. His left arm was stiff. He felt weak as a kitten.

"Breakfast," Levi said.

The rancher helped Zach to sit up. It was then he realized he was in his long red underwear under the blankets. His face reddened in the light of the morning sun that was blazing through the window.

"Where are my clothes?"

"Well, Leroy and me, we put you to bed some time ago. Now get ready for this tray. Sally fixed it up."

As Zach ate hungrily, Levi settled in the chair.

"You took a chance, Zach, headin' off those rustlers when Sally was with you."

"I told her to stay where she was safe."

"Well, now you know. She don't do nothin' you tell her."

"Worst thing, I lost my horse."

"You pick out any one we got, and it's yours."

"Thanks."

As Zach finished eating, there was a knock downstairs. They heard Sally's lilting voice greeting someone. Levi took the tray of empty plates while Zach retained his coffee cup.

"Has to be the sheriff," Levi said. "You stay right where you are. I'll be back soon."

Levi left with the tray, and Zach sipped his coffee. He felt weak and grimy, wishing he could have a good bath. He heard voices downstairs but couldn't catch the words.

Before long, Jed Long and Levi entered the room. The sheriff pulled up a chair, and Levi stood near him.

"Not one of them rustlers had any papers on 'em," Jed told him. "They was all strangers. That makes me figger they was paid to run off them cattle."

Levi folded his arms. "Could be the small ranchers put 'em up

51

to it just to keep me busy so I wouldn't be crowdin''em. Tealman maybe."

"Well, there's a dance cornin' up in a few weeks," Jed said, "and all of you will be thrown together. Now, I'm warnin' you and the Tealmans and everyone else. Anyone gets out of hand, me and Zach, we're throwin''em in jail."

"My boys will behave," Levi promised.

"I'm talkin' about you."

Levi grinned. "All right, Jed. You got my word. But this young fellow in bed here, I ain't sure he'll be in shape for any dance."

"I'll be there," Zach responded. "I like to kick up my heels same as any man."

Jed folded his arms. "I saw Primo out by the corral lookin' like a mad rooster. You watch yourself, Zach."

They left him to rest.

While Zach was sleeping, Simon Oliver was sitting behind his huge walnut desk in the well-polished office at the bank. A big window with velvet curtains gave a view of the street. His long face was deep in thought.

He was shuffling papers, but his mind was on Sally.

A knock at the door brought an elderly male clerk inside with a letter.

"Another one from that Fletcher Dannack fellow," the clerk said. "This time it's from Kansas."

Simon waited until the man was gone before slowly opening the letter, staring at the words. His face darkened, his mouth tight, lines deepening in his handsome face.

Then Simon crumpled the letter in his hand.

SIX

Zach had slept all afternoon, and when he awakened, it was nearly dark outside the Scofield ranch house. He heard no sounds, but he could smell something cooking downstairs.

He was feeling stronger, and looked around for his clothes in the pale lamplight. His holster was hanging on the post next to him, but where were his britches? There was a closet in the corner. He slid out of bed, pausing as a dizzy spell swept him momentarily. He scratched his long red underwear and thought about a bath. Still a bit dazed, he turned up the lamp on the dresser.

Opening the closet door, he peered inside.

His shirt and britches had been washed and pressed. He hardly recognized them. His boots had been wiped clean. Taking the clothes over his arm and his boots in hand, he turned around and stared in dismay at Sally Scofield.

Apron over a calico dress, her crimson hair pinned away from her face, she was standing there in surprise. His face redder than his underwear, Zach jumped back inside the closet, pulling the door closed. There was little room, and it was pitch-dark, so he opened the door a crack.

"Zach Lassiter, you come out of there and get back in bed."

"I ain't cornin' out with you there."

"I've got two brothers, Zach."

"I ain't cornin' out."

"I just wanted to tell you I have a hot bath for you. Right down the hall in the next room. But I should help you get there. You know you're not strong enough."

"Just get."

She laughed. "For a brave man, you sure are bashful."

He heard the door close, and he peered out of the closet. She was gone. His face was burning with embarrassment, and he hurriedly pulled on his britches.

Then he sneaked out to have his bath in the old iron tub. It felt mighty good, but when he pulled his clothes on, his left arm hurt so bad he could hardly get it through a sleeve. Then he replaced the sling. He was still weak and a bit dizzy, but he was also hungry.

Downstairs, he found Levi and his sons just entering the front door. They stared at him in surprise.

"Well," Luke said, "you'll be good and clean for your ride back to town."

"He's staying here until he's well," Sally said from the dining-room door.

Zack's face was deep pink, and he refused to look at her. He was still weak, but he was too busy being embarrassed to think about his wound.

Leroy teased Zach all through supper. Levi was talking about more rustler activity, trying to get Zach to stick around. Luke was grumpy. Sally was smiling and trying to catch Zach's eye. She had seen him in his underwear, and he was still red-faced.

"I sent Primo and some of the boys to the west line shack," Levi said to Zach. "That should keep him out of your hair for a few weeks. I promised the men they could draw straws to see who could go to the dance, so if he's there, you got to watch yourself."

Later, the men sat around the hearth with a small fire blazing, and Levi talked of the old days. Even after his sons went up to bed, he was telling Zach about his longtime war with the Mescalero.

"Funny thing is," the rancher added, "I got a lot of respect for 'em. Ain't no better fighter than an Apache."

"I scouted for the Army down in Arizona for about a year, and I sure would agree with you," Zach said.

They talked late into the night, Zach enjoying every minute with the rancher.

When Zach retired to his room, he found the lamp burning low and his bed all made up, which was rather pleasant. A man could get used to being spoiled, he thought. He turned up the lamp and noticed how clean the room had become.

Still weak, he went to the bed and sat down.

"I knew you were dizzy."

He turned to stare at Sally in the doorway. She looked very friendly, her dark eyes flashing in the pale light.

"Don't you ever knock?" he grunted, standing.

"Sit down, Zach." She came over as he sat again on the bed, and she adjusted his sling.

He looked up at her, too weary to stand, but enjoying her nearness. "You sure worry about me."

She drew back. "Well, it's only because you don't have any common sense."

Zach staggered to his feet and towered over her. "Now, you listen to me, Miss Sally Scofield. I can take care of myself."

"Sit down, Zach."

They were standing rather close, and he was beginning to feel a need to reach for her with his one good arm. Yet he was unsteady, and weaving.

She reached out to seize him at the waist. "Zach, you're going to fall. Please sit down. I knew you should have stayed in bed."

Any man who didn't grab an opportunity like this was a fool, and Zach was pretty bright. He swayed forward.

She tried to steady him, even as his right arm slid around her and pulled her against him. Startled, she looked up into his clear blue eyes. His breath was warm on her pink face. He weaved a little, as if he were going to fall.

"Zach, please, sit down."

But Zach was gazing at her rosy lips, inches from his. Her dark green eyes were round and flashing surprise. Now he pulled her closer, tighter, crushing her with his right arm.

Her left hand had slid around him at the waist, but her right was attempting to avoid his injured arm. And she wasn't pushing him away.

At the same time, she was breathless. He bent his head, his lips pressed firm and searching on hers. He wanted to hold her forever. She felt wonderful against him, and her lips were so soft, he didn't want to stop. His face was hot, his pulse racing so fast that he felt he would burst.

For a brief moment, she was kissing him back.

Zach was going crazy with her warmth.

Then suddenly she fought her way free, forcing him away. He lost his balance as he sat down on the bed, and he knew his face was reddening. She looked angry, but it was sure worth it. He found himself grinning foolishly.

"Zach, you tricked me."

"Couldn't help it."

Hands on hips, she glared at him. "Now you get into bed and stay there until I tell you different."

"Yes, ma'am."

There was a flash of a smile on her face, but she was still annoyed when she turned and left the room.

Yet as she closed the door behind her, she took a deep breath. His kiss had not been so unexpected. The surprise was the way it had left her so shaken that she could hardly walk. The wall she had built around herself had crumbled with his very touch.

Downstairs, she saw her father sitting alone in front of the fire.

"What is it, Sally?"

Her face was rosy as she moved to sit on the arm of his big leather chair, sliding her hand into his.

"Oh, that Zach. He's a lot of trouble."

"But you like him."

"Yes, but how can I trust any man, Father?"

"Zach's a man, Sally, in every sense of the word. Now that Fletcher, he had something missing. You just didn't know it. And if you can't see the difference between 'em, I ain't learned you nothin'."

"And?"

"You askin' if I approve of him makin' cow eyes at you?"

"Yes."

"Honey, you're the only daughter I got. I don't figure any man's good enough for you, but he comes close."

"And Simon Oliver?"

Levi shrugged. "He's a hard-working, respectable man.

"But?"

"I'm an old-timer, Sally. I relate better to a roughand-tumble man like Zach, because he's a lot like me, but that don't mean Simon wouldn't be better for you. Men like me and Zach, we don't live that long." Sally rested her head on his shoulder.

But late the next afternoon, she protested Zach's getting out of bed and helplessly watched him saddle one of the ranch horses at the corral. It was a big black that kept nudging him.

"Where do you think you're going, Zach?"

"I'm going to town."

"I'll go with you."

He turned around and walked up close to her. The wind was blowing her soft hair about her face and throat. The calico dress didn't do her justice. She backed away a step.

"It's time you did as you were told," Zach said. "No man tells me what to do."

"And what if you get hitched?"

"If I was to marry, and I say *if,* I would listen to what he had to say."

"And that's all?"

She put her chin higher in the air. "Yes."

He grinned, pushing his hat back from his brow. "I figure it's time we had that shooting match."

She frowned. "Maybe. But you are not riding into town alone. You lost a lot of blood, Mr. Lassiter."

Leroy was coming out of the house, and Zach nodded to him. "Don't worry. Leroy's cornin' with me."

She spun around and headed for the house, passing the grinning Leroy, who caught her arm and turned her about.

"Hey, Sis, what's happening between you and Zach?"

"He's stubborn."

"And you ain't?"

She had to smile, then laugh. "Just see he doesn't fall off his horse."

On the way to town, Leroy entertained Zach with his stories. The late-afternoon sun was warm, and it was one mighty pleasant ride.

In town, Leroy went to the saloon and Zach headed for the boardinghouse, where he found Emily knitting in the parlor. Two old men were playing checkers in the comer, but were ending their game. She appeared nervous and surprised to see him, and he was curious.

But she wasn't wearing black. Her dress was light green with dark velvet trim. She had curled her blond hair, and her face was flushed. She didn't look like any widow.

The two old men went up the stairs, and Zach was alone with Emily.

"Everything all right?" he asked, sitting down near her.

"Yes, of course. And you're still wearing that badge. Honestly, Zach, don't you know that lawmen don't live very long? And it's not that respectable an occupation. If you want to win some lady's hand, you need to change your way of life, find something different to do."

"Like bein' a gunsmith?"

She bit her lip, then nodded. "All right, so that's still bothering you. Yes, it's true, Zach. I chose Ricky because he would give me a better life, and I wouldn't have to sit up all night wondering if my husband was still alive. Was that so wrong?"

"Not if you loved Ricky."

"I loved you both."

"Well, that was a long time ago, and I ain't here to change your mind about anything. I'm lookin' to find out who murdered Ricky, and that's all."

He realized he was punishing her, and he was sorry. "Why don't you let it go, Zach? You'll just get hurt, and it won't change anything. Ricky's dead."

"That's it?"

"I'm ready to make a new life."

"Well, I ain't forgettin' so easy."

"What are you doin' here?" a man's voice boomed. Zach stood up and turned to see Luke Scofield walking into the room. The man was wearing a fine new coat and looked very angry, his boyish face twisted and darkened. His hand was resting on his holster.

Emily stood up slowly, her face rosy. "Luke Scofield, I presume you know Zachariah Lassiter? He was Ricky's brother."

"Yeah, I know 'im. My Pa wants him for a hired hand."

Zach ignored him and stood up, turning to Emily. "Seems like you were expectin' Luke here."

"Well, yes, but it's all very proper, Zach."

Luke grinned as Zach walked past and out of the room. But in the hallway, another man had just entered with a bunch of red roses in his hand. It was Ray Tealman, all fancied up in a new coat, and startled to see Zach.

60

"Well, I reckon I ain't the first," Tealman said. "No, the parade's just started."

"I ain't figured you out yet, Lassiter. But when I do, I don't reckon I'm gonna like you much. And that badge don't change nothin'."

Zach grinned, but alone outside in the twilight, he drew a deep breath. He was plenty annoyed.

Not at Luke, who apparently had designs on Emily, since single women were outright scarce. Not even at Luke's insulting manner, because it was obviously jealousy. Nor at Ray Tealman, another suitor who must have felt mighty silly with those roses in hand.

Zach was annoyed with Emily. He had seen more in her face than embarrassment. He had read guilt, and that bothered him. Biting his lip, he headed down the alley.

Right now, he'd sure like to run into Leroy and hear the young man's laughter. As Zach came around the hotel, he saw the sheriff coming up the street.

"Well, everyone's beatin' a path to the widow," Jed said with a smile.

"You ever see Luke Scofield or Ray Tealman call on her before?"

"No, I haven't. Why?"

"I'm just tryin' to put the pieces together. You seen Leroy?"

"Over at the Lucky Lady. And there's some of Tealman's hands in there, so maybe we oughta keep an eye on him."

They were starting to cross the street when they heard a shot. They both listened and waited. The twilight had turned to darkness. A few lamps were burning in front of stores, but the street was empty.

Two men came out of the Lucky Lady and looked around, then went back inside. Zach and the sheriff crossed over and entered the busy, smoke-filled saloon. Men were playing cards and some were crowded around the tables watching.

The chubby bartender greeted them over the piano music.

Jed leaned on the bar. "You hear a shot?"

"Out back, I think. But you know how it is, sheriff. The boys like to shoot at the moon."

Zach looked around. There was no sign of Leroy.

He followed the sheriff out the back door, closing it on the noise and smoke. They stood in the starlight, allowing their eyes to become accustomed to the night. It was cold, with no wind.

Behind the saloon were shacks and tents. They could see lamps burning. They could hear some laughter. There was music, and a woman was singing. The night seemed mighty peaceful. He wondered if Leroy had wandered into the tent city to see some woman.

The sheriff drew his six-gun and turned to walk to the alley to their left, and Zach walked around to the right.

Hand on his holster, Zach felt a cold chill running up his back.

SEVEN

Behind the Lucky Lady Saloon, the noise from the tent city was the only sound. Zach entered the alley, walking slowly, then halting. There was a man lying face down in the dirt. Zach felt his stomach reeling with recognition.

When the sheriff joined him, Zach was already kneeling. "Leroy, blast it, wake up."

Zach drew back, blood on his hand. The sheriff got on one knee beside him and struck a match. Leroy had been shot in the back between the shoulder blades. Zach wiped his hand in the dirt, but he was angry and choked up, barely able to talk.

He sprang to his feet and ran back behind the saloon, Jed at his heels. They spread out through the tents and shacks, looking, listening, sprays of lamplight and the rising moon guiding them. Silence fell suddenly, and the tents and shacks went dark.

Zach stood quiet, listening, then spun around, on instinct.

A bullet screamed by his head, and he dived for the dirt near a tent. Another shot hit the dust in front of him. Jed had knelt behind some crates some twenty feet away.

They heard running feet beyond the tents, and Zach sprang to his feet.

"Wait!" Jed warned. "You'll run into a bullet!"

But Zach went racing along the dark comers of the tent city. He could hear horses snorting. As he rounded a shack, another bullet whistled by his shoulder.

He dived behind the building, out of breath. He could hear horses. He drew a deep breath, then jumped up and ran around the shack. He saw two men swinging astride the nervous animals.

Zach charged forward, and both fired at him, one shot creasing his left arm. Zach fired back several times. One man gasped and twisted in the saddle, then fell crazily to the ground. The other man was hit but kept firing, one bullet knocking off Zach's hat, the other singeing his shoulder.

Zach dived for the dirt, rolled over, and fired. The man was hit, but spun his horse and charged Zach.

Leaping to his feet, Zach stepped aside and grabbed the man's boot, shoving him bodily into the air and out of the saddle. The horse danced and spun around as Zach fought to get over to the man, who dropped his rifle, jumped to his feet, and pulled a six-gun, blood trickling down his arm.

"Your gun's empty, Lassiter."

Zach saw the gleaming eyes and yellow teeth as the big man sneered and started to pull the trigger. Zach leaped aside as the man fired, but another shot rang out, and the man went wild-eyed, clutching his chest and letting out a cry that echoed in the night.

Out of breath, Zach watched the man crumple to the ground. Jed came running up, his six-gun still smoking.

"You all right, Zach?"

"Yeah, just a crease."

"You sure took a chance."

"Know 'em?"

Jed turned both men over in the moonlight. "Nope."

"Well, they knew me."

There were no papers on the men, which frustrated Zach. They turned back, walking slowly to the alley. Zach tied his bandanna around his arm, but the wound was not serious.

With tears brimming in his eyes, Zach knelt by Leroy in the alley as the sheriff lit a match. "He was just a foolish kid. Who would wanta kill 'im?" Zach asked.

Jed shrugged. "He got in somebody's way, that's for sure."

Zach lifted the youth in his arms and stood up, swaying under the weight. The sheriff led the way behind the saloons until they could cut across to the undertaker's. Zach thought of Ricky, and it was all the more painful.

When they left that building, Jed Long turned to Zach in the light of the rising moon. "One of us has to tell the Scofields."

Zach swallowed hard. "Luke's over at the boardinghouse. I'll let you take care of him while I ride on out."

"You could let Luke tell 'em."

"He may wanta stay in town with his brother. No, I'll ride to Antler."

But all the way back to the ranch that night, Zach kept wondering how he was going to tell Levi and Sally.

Seeing Leroy murdered had meant more than the loss of a friend. It had been like a knife in Zach's gut, reminding him that his brother Ricky had died a slower death.

Back at the ranch, he rode up to the bunkhouse and called

Oscar outside to tell him. The foreman was shattered by the news and could barely talk.

With Oscar following on foot, Zach rode up to the main house, where lights were still burning. He dismounted, feeling a chill from the night.

They removed their hats and knocked on the door. Levi let them in, admitting he had been sleeping in his leather chair in front of the blazing fire.

Sally was coming down the stairs in a blue dressing gown that flowed softly about her. She looked like a princess missing only the jewelry and crown in her long red hair. Zach stared at her a long moment.

"Zach, I'm glad you're here. Are you all right?"

"Yeah, I'm fine."

"Didn't Leroy come back with you?"

He felt all warmth leave his skin. He couldn't look at her any longer and went to Levi, who had returned to his chair and sprawled out, rubbing his eyes.

"Father, were you dreaming again?"

Sally came to sit on the arm of Levi's chair and put her hand on his. Zach stood a long moment, unable to speak. But Levi looked at him, and suddenly knew something was wrong.

"What is it, Zach?"

Slowly, Zach sat down on a chair.

Sally was frightened. "Has something happened to Leroy?"

"He's dead. The sheriff and I heard a shot. We found him in the alley by the Lucky Lady. Shot in the back. We got the ones that done it, but they had no papers. They knew me, but we didn't know them."

Levi gasped, his face white. Sally put her hand to her mouth, smothering her cry. She slid onto Levi's lap and hugged him as she sobbed and wept. The rancher held her tight, but his gaze was on Zach as tears filled his eyes.

"Where's Luke?"

"He was up at the boardinghouse, callin' on the widow Lassiter. The sheriff was goin' to tell him while I rode out here. I reckon he's with his brother right now."

"Who'd wanta kill my boy?" Levi murmured. "They startin' to pick us off, are they?"

Zach swallowed hard, knowing no way to comfort them.

It was a sad time at the Scofield ranch. The funeral was held in town at the church, and Leroy was buried not far from Ricky Lassiter. Nearly the whole town was there.

A few days later, Zach spent a lot of time covering the country, even calling on the Tealman ranch, where he wasn't particularly welcome, although Ray Tealman wasn't home. One of the Tealman hands showed him the cottonwoods where Ricky had been lynched. It had been painful, and Zach was haunted by it.

Then the Friday of the dance arrived. It was a big event, with a barbecue scheduled for Saturday, followed by horse races and a shooting match. Settlers and ranchers had come from miles around. There were visitors from Lincoln, Mesilla, and Socorro.

The dance was held in the town hall on the east side of town, near the church. Wagons and buggies were all over the street and behind the buildings. Women were in their finery, and men wore their Sunday best.

Fiddlers collected on the small stage. The music was swift, wild, and beautiful. The dancers filled the hall and bumped into one another, laughing and singing along with the music.

Zach entered and joined Oscar at the punch table, the only

open space. He could see a subdued Sally dancing with her father, then with Simon, then with a dozen others anxious to cut in and swing her in their arms. It had been weeks since the funeral, but she was obviously thinking of her loss and not the surrounding laughter. In a blue satin dress, she was breathtaking.

Levi was dancing with Ma Rindell, who was giggling at his jokes, but he soon came over to join Zach and Oscar. "Man, my boots sure hurt about now. Ain't you fellas dancing? Sure helps a man forget his troubles."

Zach saw Emily and Luke whirling about the floor, with Ray Tealman chasing them and trying to cut in. Emily wore green and white lace and looked right pretty.

Sally was dancing now with Primo, who was trying to hold her tight. She looked frightened and was pushing him away. Primo appeared to have been drinking heavily.

Levi's face darkened, and he started to move.

"I'll take care of it," Zach told him.

The music stopped, but Primo held on to her, ignoring other men who tapped his shoulder. Sally was trying to get free. Zach approached through the crowd.

The music started again with a waltz, and Primo was trying to make Sally dance. Zach laid a hard grip on the gunman's shoulder, jerking him aside.

Primo kept his left hand on Sally's arm as he glared at Zach. "Get away from me, Lassiter."

"It's my dance."

Sally was breathless, staring at each of them.

"Listen to me, Lassiter, she promised this next dance to me, and you ain't interferin'."

Zach reached over and grabbed Primo's left wrist, jerking it from Sally's arm and shoving Primo aside. The crowd fell back and away, startled.

Primo regained his balance, his right hand near his holster. "All right, Lassiter. You got lucky once before, but you ain't gonna be lucky this time."

"Outside," someone shouted. "There's women and children in here."

"Outside it is," Primo snarled.

Zach nodded. "You first."

Primo stormed toward the door, and Sally gasped. "No, Zach."

But Zach was already following the gunman. Oscar, Levi, and Luke led the way onto the boardwalk as Zach and Primo moved into the street, walking between the wagons.

The night was dark and cold, and plenty damp. There was no moon, but the stars were bright.

Zach walked around a buggy and turned to face Primo, but the man was already drawing.

Leaping aside as a bullet burned his ear, Zach pulled his six-gun and dropped behind a wagon, firing at Primo's running legs. He slit the man's trouser at the thigh.

Primo yelled and got down behind a trough, his hat visible. "You're dead, Lassiter."

"Come out and fight like a man, Primo."

The gunman fired again, the bullet crashing into the wagon wheel, the team snorting and jerking about. Zach knelt lower and looked to his left. The men on the boardwalk had retreated inside the door. There was no sign of the sheriff.

Primo was moving around behind the trough.

"I'm gonna kill you, Lassiter."

Zach didn't move. The wagons afforded a great deal of

marginal cover in all directions, but the trough was solid in front of Primo, who had to be lying on his side.

Firing swiftly, Zach hit Primo's hat, which went sailing down the boardwalk. Primo muttered under his breath and cowered out of sight.

Zach stood up suddenly and charged the trough.

Primo fired frantically and missed. Zach holstered his Colt, leaped over the trough, and landed on top of the gunman. Primo fired again, but Zach was all over him, pounding him with his fists. Primo fought back with great strength.

They broke apart, leaping to their feet, facing each other with fists ready, dancing around like roosters. Primo had some blood on his thigh. Zach's left arm was aching from his old wound.

Zach slammed his fist into the man's jaw. Primo's head shot back, but he punched and beat on Zach, knocking him backward. Zach fought back, shoving his fist into Primo's gut. The gunman doubled up with a gasp, but recovered to hammer at Zach's face.

Then Zach hit the man on the jaw again. Primo lost his balance and dropped to his knees, grabbing at air. Zach slammed his fists into his jaw and body, again and again. Primo's head snapped back several times, but he cursed, scrambling to his feet and charging.

"Two bits on Lassiter," someone shouted from a window.

The two men grappled, both drenched with sweat and out of breath, trying to pound each other in the clinch, but Zach suddenly whammed his fist into Primo's gut. Primo doubled up and let go of Zach.

Dropping to his knees again, Primo was done.

It was then that Jed Long appeared with a shotgun.

"You're a little late," Zach said, gasping for air.

"Who started it?"

Levi came onto the boardwalk. "Primo."

"Well, come along, Primo. You're gonna sleep it off."

"I ain't goin' to no jail," Primo snarled.

But Jed marched him off down the street. Zach wiped his face with his bandanna. He figured he had earned a dance with Sally, but he was a mess. Sitting down on the boardwalk with his boots in the dirt, he fought for breath. Oscar reached over and put Zach's hat back on.

Levi knelt at his side. "Well done, Zach."

"He ain't finished with you," Oscar warned.

"Nor am I," a sweet voice said.

Zach turned and looked up at Sally. He managed to stand up and remove his hat. "Sorry if I spoiled your dance."

"Come along, Zach," she said, taking his arm.

Meekly, still exhausted and breathing hard, he let her lead him back inside the hall, where the music had started up again. They were playing a waltz. He faced her a bit awkwardly. Then she put her left hand on his shoulder and slid her right hand into his left.

He hesitated, staring down at her.

Then he swung into the waltz, which he had learned long ago from Emily. With his right arm around Sally, he moved her about with grace, and she was smiling up at him in surprise.

"You're a brave man, Zach Lassiter."

He couldn't answer. Dancing with this beautiful woman was so overwhelming that he couldn't do anything but hold her and sway across the floor. A man would be a fool not to dwell in her smile, the warmth of her, the soft scent of lilac. Her dark red hair was gleaming in the lamplight, and her green eyes were shining.

Simon Oliver suddenly tapped him on the shoulder. Zach kept dancing. Simon, his face red with anger, followed and tapped again. Reluctantly, Zach stopped and watched Sally being taken away.

She looked back over her shoulder with a smile, but Simon whirled her into the crowd of dancers.

Retreating to the punch table, Zach was confronted by Emily, who moved closer to him.

"You haven't asked me to dance, Zach."

"I ain't much of a dancer."

"I taught you to dance, remember? And I saw you with Sally Scofield. I'm wondering if you're avoiding me. I thought we had something once, you and me." No one was around, and Zach could contain his questions no longer. She looked as if she might be able to answer them now. He watched her face as he spoke. "Where were you the night Ricky was killed?"

"I told you, I was waiting supper until after midnight."

"Sheriff said you weren't home when he went by there at nine o'clock, said there was no answer and he pounded plenty loud on the door."

She stared at him, her face turning several shades of red, and she backed away, her hand to her throat, unable to answer. Guilt lurked in her brown eyes. "Well?" Zach demanded.

Before she could answer, Luke was at her side and drawing her away, giving Zach a dirty look. Emily was shattered and could barely walk.

Zach was angry. She was hiding something, all right. He couldn't breathe. He walked outside, where Levi was leaning against a post and staring into the moonlight. He forgot about Emily when he saw the strange look on the rancher's face.

"You all right, Levi?"

"I was thinkin' of Leroy. Who'd wanta kill him?"

"Who'd want to kill my brother?"

"There's somethin' more than rustlin' goin' on here, Zach, and I don't like it. You figure Dannack's got somethin' to do with it?"

A sudden shot hit Levi in the right chest, and he gasped, staggering forward and sinking to his knees, his body shuddering. The shot's echo rang in the cold of the night, the music halting inside and leaving a sudden silence.

Zach spun around with his six-gun in hand.

EIGHT

Zach shoved Levi down behind a wagon and knelt, six-gun ready. The moon had come out, filling the street with its glow. Behind them, the music had stopped, and people were crowding the door and windows.

"Get back," Zach snarled at them.

Levi was hurt bad, curled up and unable to talk. Zach moved around the wagon, looking, watching. He saw nothing. Luke came darting out of the doorway and dropped to his father's side.

"Pa!"

Sally came running forward, and Zach leaped up, grabbing her arm and throwing her bodily down to where Luke was kneeling over Levi. She gasped and fell on her brother.

Zach peered across the street and up and down the boardwalks. There was no sound, no movement. The hush surrounding them was so still he could have heard a man swallow.

Jed was suddenly running up the street in the shadows of the buildings. He reached them and knelt beside Zach.

Luke got up and went in to drag the doctor out of the hall and over to Levi. Sally was holding her father's hand, no color in her face. Levi was still doubled up in terrible pain.

Jed turned to Zach. "I'll cross over to the alley between the cafe and the Lucky Lady. Cover me."

Zach looked down at Levi, then turned. "No, you cover me."

Zach sprang to his feet and darted across the street and into the alley. As he reached the cover, he heard running feet behind the saloon. With a surge of energy, Zach charged out of the alley and around the building. He could see a man already behind the livery and still running.

Running full speed, six-gun in hand, Zach fought for breath and covered the distance in record time. As he neared the livery, a shot rang out from a crack in the boards, high in the loft, striking him high on his left shoulder, above the collarbone, creasing him.

Gasping and falling aside, Zach realized he had been set up. He dropped to the ground, rolling toward the back wall of the livery. Bullets spat on the ground and dug in around him. His wound hurt plenty, and he could feel the hot blood trickling down inside his shirt.

Jed came running from the street and along the wall, darting and dodging, then falling next to Zach.

"Two in the loft," Zach said. "Another at the corrals."

"You stay here."

"Not a chance. I'll take the ones inside."

"You can't move fast enough."

"Wanta bet on it?"

Jed grinned. "All right, but give me time to get to the corrals so I can distract 'em. I'll get back around as soon as I can."

Zach moved toward the front of the livery, keeping close to the wall. Jed went carefully around the back.

As Zach neared the large open doors in front of the barn, he heard the gunfire in the corrals. Quickly, he scooted inside the doors and dived into the straw piles near the stalls. The first horse snorted at his intrusion.

Lamps hung inside the front door and gave some light through the stall area. The loft ran along both sides of the barn, and the ladder to the loft hung near the rear entrance.

Zach crawled along the front of the stalls. A big bay stallion had a double-walled stall with a boarded-up front, but the horse could reach down and quickly took a bite at Zach's rear as he passed. Zach was startled and turned around to give the animal a dirty look, then paused. It had a handsome head with a white star, and its mane was white. It snorted at him.

Zach turned and kept crawling, ignoring his pain. There was more gunfire at the corral.

He could see two men in the loft. They were on their knees, peering out the window. There was more gunfire outside. Zach wondered if Jed was just firing his gun to keep them distracted.

There was a space now that Zach had to cross with no cover. He swallowed hard, praying the men would not turn. He got to his feet and ran along the stalls, startling two horses that danced and snorted.

He knew the men were alerted as he dived into an empty stall and rolled over. Bullets crashed into the boards around him. He got to his knees, peering past the stall. He could see that the men were lying down in the loft, trying to get a shot at him.

The outside gunfire stopped, and Zach lay still.

Suddenly one of the men reared up with a rifle, and Zach

fired, hitting him dead center. The man cried out, then screeched and rolled off the edge of the loft, hitting the ladder on the way down and crashing to the dirt floor in a heap, jerking as he died.

Zach waited, knowing the other man was moving through the loft to find a better position. Now he could see his hat, halfway toward the front of the barn, moving quickly.

Then the man got up on one knee and aimed with his rifle, the bullets spinning by Zach, who fired back, hitting the man in the forehead.

Stunned, the man rolled over.

Zach got to his feet and went to the ladder, but Jed came running inside.

"Well, you got both of 'em, Zach. Ain't never seen 'em before. Mine got away, but he was hit bad. I'm gonna saddle up and try to catch 'im. Can you make it over to the doc okay?"

"Yeah, but watch yourself."

Zach shoved his bandanna inside his shirt as Jed ran out the back doorway. Slowly, the numbness at his collarbone sending shock waves through him, Zach headed for the front entrance.

But he paused to stare at the stallion. It tossed its head and bit at him. Zach grinned and reached for the horse's nose, but it shook its head free.

Zach turned to see Luke slipping inside the front door, then straightening when he saw that the fight was over.

"Zach, you all right?"

"I got two. Jed's trailing the other. How's your pa?"

"I don't know. He's at Doc's. Maybe I'd better go with Jed."

"If you can catch him."

Luke ran through the livery and out the back door, shouting the sheriff's name. Jed called from the corral.

Zach headed out of the livery barn, a bit unsteady on his feet. He leaned on the wall as he heard the horses leaving out back.

Down the street at the town hall, people were milling around on the boardwalk. He started across. The bleeding had stopped but his wound stung something fierce.

Sally came running, unmindful of her pretty dress, and caught his right arm. "Zach Lassiter, you're hurt."

Not missing the chance, Zach slid his right arm around her shoulders, leaning on her. She sure smelled good. He pretended to be more hurt than he was.

Simon Oliver came forward, forcing a look of concern on his long face. He grabbed Zach's other arm. "It's okay, Sally, I've got him."

But Zach kept his arm around Sally, which annoyed the already jealous Simon.

"How's Levi?" Zach asked.

"He's with the doctor," she said.

Other men came forward as Zach told them Luke and Jed were after the third gunman.

Ray Tealman on their heels, Simon and Sally helped Zach down the street to the doctor's office, which was next to the hotel. Lamplight gleamed through the curtains.

Inside, they found Levi stretched out on a long table, his shirt off and his chest bandaged. His eyes were closed. The doctor turned to them.

"How is he?" Sally asked, anxious.

"I can't tell yet."

Zach was settled down into a chair, and the doctor came to look at him, peeling off his vest and bloody shirt, as well as folding down the top of his red underwear.

Sally went to her father, leaning over to kiss him.

Ray Tealman and Simon Oliver stood aside, watching. Zach studied them as the doctor cleansed his wound.

Simon had an interest in Sally. With her father and brothers out of the way, he'd have the whole ranch. Tealman, he had set his sights on Emily, but with the Scofields out of the way, he could spread out onto Levi's grass.

Suddenly the doctor was applying alcohol that burned. Zach gasped, but the doctor just smiled.

"Bullet went clean through. It's just a flesh wound."

Relieved, Zach closed his eyes and drew a deep breath, his head back, and he felt a cool hand on his brow. He gazed up and saw Sally smiling at him.

The men helped Zach to his feet and walked him to a couch at the back wall, and Zach closed his eyes in sudden exhaustion.

When he awakened, it was morning. Jed was sitting in a chair watching him. Luke and Sally were asleep in chairs near their father, who was sleeping peacefully. There was no sign of the doctor or anyone else.

Zach lifted himself a little. He felt strong and the pain had eased. "Did you get 'im, Jed?"

"Luke did. But we never saw 'im before either." Luke was awakened by their voices, and he came to kneel near Zach, who nodded to him.

"Pa's sleeping. Doc thinks he'll be all right now."

"That's what I need," Jed said, rising. "Sleep."

"Hold on," Zach said. "We got to talk about this. First Leroy, then Levi. Luke, you're next."

Luke nodded. "I think you're right."

Jed stretched as he stood up. "Well, when you figure it out, let me know. I'm goin' to bed for a while. We still got the barbecue and the horse races this afternoon, and the shooting match. Crowd will be plenty big, and we got to be alert."

"By the way," Zach said, "I saw a bay stallion in the livery. Who owns it?"

Luke stood up slowly. "Why, he used to be Pa's, but he's loco. No one could ride him. And weren't nobody wanted any colts out of him because he was too mean. Pa sold him to old Ryan, who runs the livery. It's too bad, actually. I'll bet that stallion could outrun any horse in town."

"And the races are this afternoon," Zach said. "Yeah, but forget it," Luke said. "You can't ride that animal. No one can."

"Got any idea why he got so ornery?"

Luke grinned. "Well, yeah. I figure that stud's got a mind of his own. Pa got him cheap because he hadn't been broke, but ole Rocket just ain't never met nobody smarter than he is, that's all."

After Jed left the office, Luke sat on the chair, then glanced at the sleeping Sally and Levi. He folded his arms.

"Zach, I know Tealman wants our grass, but I can't see he'd be this underhanded. He's never been bashful about doin' his own handiwork."

"What about Fletcher Dannack?"

"That could explain all these strange faces, all right."

"But that don't explain who killed my brother," Zach said. "You got any ideas?"

"No."

Luke stood up and went over to his father, taking the wet cloth and wiping the man's brow.

The doctor came out of the back room, yawning as he looked around. Then he checked Levi, who opened his eyes.

Sally got up quickly. "Father, you're awake."

Levi grunted. "Feel like I got hit by a locomotive."

"Missed your vitals," the doctor said. "You're gonna be all right."

Zach sat up, feeling normal again. His left shoulder was bandaged and stung a little. He was conscious of his bare chest, and tried to pull up his underwear to cover it. Sally came and helped him, causing him to turn beet red. Then she pulled his shirt over his right arm. She was still in her blue satin dress.

"Zach, you had a close call."

"I'm goin' to see Jed."

"No, you're not," she said. "You're not moving."

"It's all right," the doctor told her. "It was just a flesh wound."

She drew back, annoyed, and Zach grinned, letting her help him stand up. She sure looked swell in the morning. Then he left the doctor's office and headed for the livery.

Meanwhile, Simon Oliver was in his office, glaring at a rough-looking man who wore a fancy black-and-white cowhide vest and twin Colts, and had conchos on his hatband. He had a hairy face and beady eyes, and his voice was sinister. He wasn't a big man, but he came across as powerful and very dangerous. His voice was raspy.

"Well, we got one Scofield so far."

Simon was stiff and annoyed. He gripped some papers on his desk to keep his hands busy. Cultured and well-educated, Simon had limited use for men like this. He glanced toward the closed door.

"Chips, keep your voice down."

"We'll finish the old man next chance we get. And that other boy of his. But the information you're gettin' from Primo hasn't been any help. The boys are bein' picked off, and we're takin' chances, so we want more money."

"We had a deal."

"The cattle didn't bring enough. And the boys are gettin' restless. They don't like hidin' from a fight."

"And?"

"You want 'em to stick around, you have to pay more."

"Listen to me, Chips. I've already paid every one of you plenty. I want you to finish your job on the Scofield men."

"More money. Or we leave."

Simon leaned back, his thin face twisted. "All right."

"Another five hundred for eatin' money, and a five-hundred bonus to split among the men."

Simon reached in his drawer and pulled out a small metal box, counting out the greenbacks. He didn't like this man, who smelled of death.

"And don't forget," Chips added. "That five thousand for us when we finish the Scofields."

"There's one more. Five hundred to the man who kills Zach Lassiter."

Chips smiled and pushed his hat back. "I heard he was sportin' a badge around here. Well, 1 ain't afraid of him."

"Just get him. I don't care how."

NINE

Before the barbecue, Zach walked up the street toward the livery. It was mid-morning, but the sun was hot. He could see tables being set up near the town hall. Fire pits were already smoking. Sally and Emily, wearing calico, were among the women helping.

Zach reached the livery and went over to the old man called Ryan to make a deal.

"You can't ride that stallion, son."

"I'd like to try."

Ryan led the stallion from his stall, and Zach was astounded. The animal had great shoulders and strong legs. It had powerful muscles and looked plenty fast. White stockings added to its overall beauty.

And it bit at Zach.

But Zach had learned a lot from the Comanches some years back. He knew how to lay on the hands. He started stroking the animal's legs and body, slowly, firmly. The stallion tossed its head and snorted, biting at him but not connecting.

"Name's Rocket," Ryan told him.

"How much?" Zach asked, straightening.

"Well, if he could be ridden, a couple thousand. He's got good bloodlines all the way to Kentucky, but nobody wants to use him 'counta he's so mean. But since he ain't good for nothin', you can have 'im for a hundred."

"Fifty."

"Eighty."

"Done."

They shook hands, and the old man wrote up the bill of sale as Zach dug out some gold coins. Luke appeared, followed by Jed. They helped walk the stallion out into the corrals. It was sound and powerful.

Luke shook his head. "You'd better let me try it, Zach. You only got one hand."

"That's all I need."

In the warm afternoon, with the rest of the town unaware, the men saddled the stallion. As usual, the horse did nothing while preparations were made. In fact, he looked half asleep.

"It's when you hit the saddle," Luke said. "He nearly killed every man what ever got on, including me. Folks figure he's got bad blood."

Zach stroked the stallion's neck. One man held the bridle and his right ear, keeping his head up.

When Zach hit the saddle with reins in his right hand and his left arm resting at his side, the stallion threw its head down, knocking his helper aside, and Rocket left the earth, so high Zach thought they would never come back down. When they hit the ground, Rocket switched and spun, nearly unseating Zach.

He was unaware of the gathering crowd. He hurt clean through from every jump and buck and whirl.

The stallion hit the sky again, spinning before it came down, head between its forelegs, hind legs kicking toward the sun. It bucked sideways, spun and jumped, then reared and spun around again.

Rocket leaped so high, Zach was dazed.

When Rocket hit the ground, Zach went up in the air, but his boots stayed in the stirrups. He slammed down into the saddle and felt pain from his toes to his ears, but as he hit the saddle, Rocket hit the sky again.

Rocket spun and kicked as he headed back to earth.

For another ten minutes, the horse kicked and squealed and stayed in the air so long Zach feared it would never come down.

Zach was hurting all over. Sweat drenched him.

And then Rocket reared up as if to go over backward.

Zach dug in his heels, and Rocket shot straight forward, heading for the fence, spinning in an effort to wipe Zach off, but Zach kicked them away from the fence by jamming his boot against the boards.

Rocket suddenly stopped, panting, sweat on his neck.

The crowd along the fence was breathless.

And Zach couldn't breathe at all. Rocket jumped a little, then stopped, tossing his head.

"He's done," someone shouted.

But Rocket was just getting his wind. Zach was dazed, aching all over, the reins so tight in his right hand that his fingers hurt. His left shoulder was painful and bleeding again.

Suddenly Rocket hit the sky, nearly unseating Zach, and the stallion kicked and spun twice before coming down to earth, hitting so hard that Zach felt the shock up to his nose.

And then Rocket began to walk around the corral. All the buck was gone.

There was a loud cheer from the crowd along the fence, and Zach, sweat dripping off his face, looked toward them with relief and no small amount of pride.

Sally was climbing onto the top rail, her smile radiant. Luke and Jed were on either side of her.

Ryan was annoyed as he came to the gate. "You sure snookered me, Lassiter."

"Hey, Lassiter," a man called. "I got some brood mares just waitin' for tendin'. What's your fee?"

Rocket kept walking around the corral without stopping, and Zach didn't tighten the reins, nor did he let down his guard.

Then, at length, Zach reined up the stallion. He dismounted slowly, ran his hands down its damp forelegs and up its neck. Rocket just looked at him, not even taking a bite.

"You're smarter than I thought," Zach muttered.

Carefully, he mounted again. Rocket stood quiet.

The crowd cheered. Then Zach dismounted, and Luke came forward to help him unsaddle.

"Never seen anything like it," Luke said. "I reckon you ain't as useless as I thought."

"What did you think?"

Luke glanced toward the crowd and spoke quietly. "I thought you come to take Emily with you. She said she was in love with you once. I got so crazy, I couldn't see straight."

"That's why you was so unfriendly."

"So are you plannin' to marry her?"

Zach shook his head, his voice low. "I don't know how I feel about her right now. She's got some explainin' to do."

"What do you mean?"

They glanced toward the anxious, cheering crowd. Zach, reins in hand, was so tired that he could hardly walk, but he was determined to groom his new mount.

As they left the corral leading Rocket, Sally waved. She was beaming as she turned away into the crowd.

"Ole Rocket's plenty smart," Luke said. "He knows when he's winnin', and he sure knows when he ain't. You gonna race him?"

"Any competition?"

Luke nodded. "Tealman's gray stallion. And I hope you beat 'im."

Inside the livery, Zach rubbed down the animal, but he was pretty much one-handed.

Ray Tealman came over and stood watching a moment.

"All right, Lassiter, are you gonna race him tomorrow?"

"Maybe."

"Ain't no way he can beat my stallion. Yours ain't never been run."

"No, but he's smart."

"Besides, you might hit the saddle, and he might hit the sky again. He ain't broke yet. One ride ain't gonna do it, you know, and you just can't trust a horse like that. You'll never be able to trust 'im. He ain't worth nothin'."

But Rocket turned and nosed Zach's arm.

At the barbecue, there was lively fiddle music and great hunks of beef and whole potatoes. Coffee steamed from huge kettles, and the town's people and their visitors were having a great time.

Simon Oliver kept following Sally around, worried that she would find time for Zach. Tealman and Luke took turns chasing Emily, who was flirting with everyone.

In a pretty calico dress with a white apron, Sally took a moment to rest in the shade, and Simon hurriedly joined her. As much as she had enjoyed watching Zach's ride, she was pale with stress.

"How's Levi?" he asked.

"He's sitting up and acting like nothing happened. He even insists on coming to the barbecue."

"He's tough."

"What do you think will happen next, Simon?"

"What do you mean?"

"They killed Leroy and tried to murder my father."

"Maybe that's the end of it."

"No, I have a terrible feeling it's not."

"You'll be safe, Sally. I'll see to it."

She slid her hand on his. "Thank you, Simon, but it's my father and Luke I'm worried about. Someone is trying to kill all the Scofield men."

He turned her hand into his. "Sally, maybe the solution is right in front of us."

"And what is that, Simon?"

"Marry me."

Sally was caught off guard and flushed. "Why, Simon, we hardly know each other."

"If someone's trying to kill off the Scofield men, it's because they want you and the ranch. If you marry me, it would all stop."

"How do you know that?"

"I don't know, but if I'm right, it could stop the killings. So what do you say?"

She stared at him, not understanding his reasoning, but her

thoughts turned quickly to Zach Lassiter. Maybe she was a fool not to grab a man like Simon, but she became flustered.

"I don't know how to answer you, Simon."

"Well, maybe this wasn't the right time, but you think about it, please."

She nodded. He was angry with himself for rushing her, but he was pressed for time. Fletcher Dannack was on his way, and Sally had loved Fletcher a long time ago. Then there was Zach hanging around. And Simon was crazy in love with Sally.

While folks were still enjoying the barbecue, Zach went to the livery and took the stallion into a back corral. Luke was helping him. Zach wasn't sure if the stallion was as smart as he figured, and he worried the animal would be back to its old tricks. His shoulder wound ached, but the rest of his body was more painful from the jarring of his ride.

Rocket did bite at him, but Zach ran his hands up and down its forelegs and neck. He held the horse's head between his hands and talked to it long and hard, while Luke stood by, grinning.

A few men gathered at the fence, waiting.

Zach kept talking to the stallion as he and Luke saddled it. He tightened the cinch and dropped the stirrup while Luke held the bridle. Then he drew a deep breath.

The stallion's ears were laid back. Luke took tight hold on the bridle and grabbed one ear, holding the stallion's head up as best he could.

"It's going to be okay," Zach said.

The stallion didn't move as Zach put his left boot in the stirrup. Very slowly, he pulled himself up, his left hand on the reins and tight on the mane, his right hand sliding onto the horn.

He reached midair over the saddle seat, his right leg slowly crossing the saddle toward the other stirrup.

Suddenly, the stallion's head went down and its rear end went up, hind legs kicking at the sky. And Zach, caught by surprise, went backward, then forward, completely off balance. Another buck sent him flying over the stallion's neck and head.

He crashed downward, hitting the hard ground with his back and head, legs following crazily. He rolled and crumpled up, the wind knocked out of him.

Dizzy, he shook his head. And then he was startled by the soft, curious nose of the stallion on his neck.

"Blast you," he growled.

Luke was laughing. The men on the fence were laughing so hard that one of them fell off and landed on his rear.

"All right," Zach said, getting to his feet and glaring at the stallion. "So we're even."

The stallion nuzzled him. Its ears were slanting forward.

"He showed you," Luke said with a grin.

Zach muttered to himself and stiffly walked around Rocket once more. This time he mounted swiftly, but the stallion was tame as a kitten.

Zach rode Rocket around the corral a few times, then set him to a lope for a few minutes. He rode over to where Luke was watching and reined up.

"Looks to me," Luke said, "you already got a rein on 'im. Real soft mouth, all right."

"He's stiff," Zach said. "You think racin's gonna hurt 'im?"

"Are you kiddin'? That stallion can outrun anything on four legs and eat a mouth full of grass along the way. No, if Rocket's stiff, it's from tryin' to buck you off yesterday."

Zach grinned and exercised the animal some more. He was plenty stiff and sore himself, and the ache in his shoulder was annoying. After a while, he gave Rocket a short rest before the race.

There were four horses in the first race, and Zach held back because Ray Tealman's gray stallion was not in it. He saw Sally with Levi, who was perched in a chair with blankets around him, still pale but not wanting to miss anything. Jed came to wish him luck. There was Emily in the shade, waving to him.

Ray Tealman rode up for the third race, which had the biggest purse—a bag of silver worth a hundred dollars. His mount was tall and lean and full of fire, dancing and snorting around the street.

The other horses fell out of the race, but Zach rode Rocket through the crowd with a lot of men cheering him. He could hear bets being placed on both sides.

That bay ain't never run no race," one merchant was saying. "I got fifty on Tealman."

Zach looked down to see Sally standing by his left stirrup, smiling up at him. She had changed clothes and was wearing a white shirt and her riding skirt, as well as her gun belt. The sun danced on her hair and in her eyes.

"My father wishes you luck."

"And you?"

"I don't know. We haven't had our shooting match yet."

"That's about an hour before sundown, ain't it?"

She nodded. "So be ready, Zach Lassiter."

Backing away, she was smiling, even as Simon Oliver came and took her arm, leading her away. Zach frowned.

Ray Tealman rode up beside him, and the stallions started

biting at each other.

"Ready to lose, Lassiter?"

Zach grinned. "I figure you're gonna be eatin' my dust."

"This horse ain't never lost a race."

"Well, this will be a first."

Men were bringing them around to a starting position.

They were lined up ten feet apart to keep the stallions from fighting. The crowd lined the boardwalks and followed along as the two riders rode toward the starting line, a deep crease drawn in the dirt.

"Now," said an important-looking merchant, "you ride off at the gun. Follow the markers clear around the town and back up the street to this same line here. First one across wins."

Ray Tealman's stallion was dancing, afire with energy.

Rocket stood quiet, rubbing his nose on a foreleg.

The gun went off. Both horses flew forward at an even charge. They barreled down the street with dust flying in the hot sun. Past the church, they saw the markers going up around the cemetery, along a low ridge, and they followed at full speed, neck and neck.

Rocket was flying effortlessly, without urging.

They sailed around and across the creek, water splashing, then hit the main trail and headed back across the narrow bridge. Ray Tealman suddenly crowded Zach's mount to the railing, hitting Rocket with his stallion. He was trying to run Zach through the railing.

But Rocket held his ground, and the two stallions charged up Main Street toward the finish line. Fifty feet from the line, Zach dug in his heels.

"Let's go, Rocket."

The stallion burst forward like a bullet, leaving the gray behind as it neared the finish line, and bolted across alone.

The crowd cheered, and Zach let the stallion slow of his own volition. Rocket wasn't even breathing hard, and Zach leaned down to stroke his neck. He was so proud of Rocket that he was bursting with pleasure.

He turned and rode back, seeing his opponent glaring at him. As he rode alongside of Ray Tealman, the man snarled under his breath.

"So you won, but I'm warnin' you. Stay away from Emily, or you're a dead man."

Zach ignored him and rode into the cheering crowd. A wreath of flowers went around Rocket's neck, placed there by a smiling Sally. Her eyes were wide and shining.

"Zach, you surprised everyone."

"And you?"

"I knew you would win."

"Am I gonna win the shootin' match?"

She hesitated, then tried to frown. "We'll see about that."

"Don't forget, I'm namin' my prize."

"No, Zach Lassiter," she whispered, looking around to be sure no one could hear. "We have a five-dollar bet."

"You have a five-dollar bet. I get my own prize."

"Then you have to say what it is."

"No, I'm gonna surprise you."

She drew herself up. "Well, it doesn't matter, because I'm going to win."

Zach just grinned and walked over to the livery, with Rocket and Luke trailing. Inside, Luke helped Zach rub the animal down. They coddled the big bay, who seemed to be enjoying the attention.

"He's just a big baby," Luke said.

"That's his good side."

They put the stallion in a stall with a blanket on his back, and Zach turned to Luke as he pulled his hat down tight.

"Now, you listen to me, Luke. The crowd out there is pretty big, and you're a target, so you'd better watch yourself. And keep an eye on Levi."

"What about you? They set you and Jed up at the livery."

"We get paid for that."

"Someone wants a clear field to Sally, all right. And they ain't too sure about havin' the law around. And I'll wager it's Dannack."

"But he hasn't showed."

"He's here, Zach. I know it."

Rocket had cooled down, so they gave the stallion some water and grain. Then, before Zach could head for the livery door, Luke confronted him.

"You got to tell me what you meant about Emily. What unanswered questions?"

"Well, she told me that the night my brother was killed, she was waiting supper till after midnight. But the sheriff went over there about nine o'clock, and no one answered the door. Said he banged on it pretty hard."

Luke stared at him, then looked away, and then turned his back. It was a long moment before he spoke, and his voice was low. "So where was she?"

"I don't know."

"Well, if she was with someone, he couldn't have killed your brother at the same time."

Zach shrugged. "Unless he paid to have it done. Just to get a clear hand with her."

For a long moment, Luke didn't move. His back still to Zach, he straightened, then left the livery.

Zach stood gazing after him, wondering. Somebody could have been with Emily that night, making her afraid to answer the door. Was it Luke or Tealman, or someone else? And was it the man who ordered his brother's death?

Turning to the stallion, Zach stroked the great neck. His eyes burned. He had visited his brother's grave more than once. Memories of Wichita had flooded his dreams. He had to help Sally, but he could never forget for a moment why he had come to Reata.

Finally, Zach left the livery. The crowd was getting ready for the shooting match up the street across from the church. Targets were set up in front of a knoll. The first rounds were with rifles.

The only woman shooting was Sally. With a Winchester in her hands, she stood with her feet apart, refusing to look directly at Zach. Levi, still pale and weak, was placed in a chair in the shade on the church porch, where he had a view over the crowd.

Jed was keeping an eye out and not participating.

Luke got in some good shots, but Sally was better. Zach kept ahead of them, and the three soon had outdistanced everyone, including a red-faced Tealman, who retreated to hold Emily's arm. Luke was distracted, casting dirty glances at him and missing an important shot.

Now it was just Zach and Sally. They were moved back to the church steps to have more distance and make the final shots more difficult.

Only Levi could hear Zach's whisper to Sally. "Don't forget, I get to name my prize."

She glared at him. "You're going to lose, so it don't matter much."

Zach lifted his Winchester and aimed. He hit a bull's-eye. Sally did the same. They kept shooting, and finally the judge came over. He was a merchant who had become weary of the match.

"I'm thinkin' it's a tie."

"No," Sally said. "Toss some silver dollars."

"Well, Miss Sally, that's not fair," the merchant protested. "You always win on that, and maybe Mr. Lassiter won't agree to my bendin' the rules."

"Toss 'em," Zach said, grinning. "Here, I'll donate 'em out of my race winnings."

He handed some silver dollars to the judge.

The coins were tossed high into the sunlight, one at a time. Sally fired and hit. Zach did likewise. Dollars were hit and spinning. He was amazed at her skill.

Bets were being made in the crowd. Applause followed every hit. Zach was getting worried.

Then, suddenly, Sally missed.

"Oh, no," she said, so surprised that she kept staring at the coin as it hit the ground.

Zach fired and hit, and the match was over. Unaware that Levi could hear them, she turned to Zach, her chin up. "I'll pay you five dollars."

"Nope," he said. "I'm namin' my prize."

"And just what do you think it is?"

"I ain't sayin'."

"What?"

"I'll let you know when I want it."

Sally flushed with color. "Zach Lassiter, you are the most exasperating man I ever met."

Zach grinned as she stormed off, walking right into Simon Oliver, who took her arm and headed into the crowd. The merchant judge came to give Zach his prize, another sack of silver dollars.

Zach turned and realized that not only was Levi still sitting there, but he must have heard the teasing. Zach grinned foolishly. Levi didn't smile, and Zach quickly turned away.

"Now," the judge said loudly, "you men with the fast draw. This is the final contest. You got to draw and hit the target faster than I can drop this coin. I hold it straight out, count to three, and that's it."

"Hey, that ain't fair," a man complained. "We always have some easy ones first. And nobody ever wins against that blasted coin."

"Yeah, but it's gettin' dark, and we ain't got no time."

The judge patiently went through five men who could not outdraw the coin, even though they hit the target easily.

Primo came forward, looking grim and ready. He bent his knees slightly and crouched, waiting. The judge was a little nervous, but he counted three and dropped the coin.

Primo drew but the coin hit dirt before he could fire. Angry, Primo hit the bull's-eye, then insisted on another try, but he was overruled. Furious, he stormed off into the crowd.

Abruptly, a tall man in his thirties stepped out, wearing a long black coat and a new black Stetson, his thin face set with a practiced smile. He was a handsome man, a stranger, and he pushed his coat back from his holster.

"Mind if I try?"

The judge nodded. "Go ahead, mister."

It was then that Zach looked over to Sally, who had lost all color. She fell against Simon Oliver, whose arm slid around her to hold her upright. Zach knew suddenly who this stranger was.

The judge dropped the coin. The stranger fired.

And he hit the target just as the coin hit the ground. The crowd cheered, and the judge was overwhelmed.

"Mister," the judge said, "ain't nobody's ever been able to do that. Let me shake your hand. You just won. And I'd sure like to know your name."

"Fletcher Dannack."

There was a long pause.

"Wait," Luke called. "You got one more contestant."

Zach was pushed forward by Luke, and he walked uneasily over to where Fletcher had stepped aside. The judge turned to Zach, who loosened his Colt in its holster. It was getting dark. It would be hard to see the coin, much less the target.

"Are you sure?" the judge asked him. "It's gettin' awful dark now. And the moon ain't come up."

Zach looked directly at Fletcher, who smiled.

No wonder the man had fooled Sally, he thought. He was the picture of a gentleman and a scholar. His manner was polite, friendly, with no tension. It would take a lot of arrogance for such a man to forget his prison term and pretend his pardon had erased everything.

Zach stood by the judge, who held the coin straight out as before. "Zach, it's dark."

"Go ahead."

The judge reluctantly counted to three, then dropped the

coin. Zach drew and fired, his hand moving so fast it was a blur. He hit the bull's-eye before the coin hit the ground, faster than Dannack had.

There was a startled hush, then a lot of cheering.

The judge was astounded. "Well, that's a tie. And I reckon we had better split the prize money."

The darkness was touched by starlight. Someone had lit lanterns by the street, their eerie light casting the shadows of the men toward the targets.

After counting out the silver to each man, the judge wearily called it a night. Zach turned to look directly at Fletcher, but the man's eyes were searching the crowd, which was wandering away. Sally and Simon were gone.

"Just passin' through?" Zach asked.

Fletcher glanced at Zach's badge and nodded. "After I rest up, maybe. I like this country. Might want to start a business here. But I ain't never met my match before. Mind if I ask your name?"

Before Zach could answer, Jed came over to them. "All right, Dannack. We know why you're here."

"Why, Sheriff, you're jumping to conclusions."

"That pardon don't make you welcome."

"So you know about the false arrest."

Jed was grim. "All I know is, you go anywhere near Sally Scofield, I'm gonna lock you up for botherin' her."

Fletcher smiled. "I think the lady should make that decision, don't you?"

Luke had come over to them, his right arm around Levi. The older man could barely stand, but his eyes were like hot coals.

"I'm Levi Scofield, and this is my son, Luke. The sheriff speaks for us. And you ain't welcome at Antler."

"I'm a patient man," Fletcher said. "When you see what a good citizen I am, you'll change your mind." Abruptly, Sally and Simon appeared at Levi's side, and she was staring at Fletcher. She came slowly forward a step or two, then paused, her eyes wide. Lamplight gleamed on her hair and face.

"Fletcher, is it true? You were pardoned?"

He bowed with a sweep of his hat. "Miss Sally, you are lovelier than ever. New Mexico becomes you." While Simon, Levi, and Zach stood helpless, Sally took another step closer, as if she could not clearly see the man.

"Why were you pardoned?"

"The witness had been paid to lie about me. At the second trial, he tried to get money from my lawyer to give true testimony, and there were witnesses. The judge was furious, but the man disappeared before they could arrest him."

"Are you saying you were innocent?"

"Sally, that's why I got a full pardon. I'm the same man you were going to marry. I came here praying you would understand."

Simon came up and took her arm. She leaned on him as she spoke. "I don't know, Fletcher."

"Then take your time, Sally. I still love you, and I know in your heart you still love me. I'm a patient man. I plan to open a business in Reata. Perhaps we can talk when you're more comfortable with me." Levi growled. "Not if I can help it."

Fletcher smiled and bowed again. "If I remember right, sir, Miss Sally has a mind of her own. But I'm hoping you will someday realize I'm an innocent man who just wants to live a normal life and be a good husband."

With that, Fletcher Dannack donned his hat and walked away. Luke held his weary father to his side, and Zach came over to help him.

Sally backed away, Simon holding her arm. She leaned on him, and he spoke softly as they stepped away from the others to be alone.

"You were going to marry that man?"

"Yes," she whispered.

"Do you still love him?"

"I don't know."

"You must feel something."

"I'm remembering how it was. Before he was arrested. And I think I owe him some loyalty, Simon. We were very happy then. I must give him a chance to prove himself."

"And if he does?"

"Then I'll know."

Simon drew a deep breath, but his face was still red. Luke and Levi came over to join them. Sally took her father's arm to help him, and with Zach trailing, they headed toward the hotel.

Simon stood staring after them. In his jealousy and anger, he took her words very seriously. He knew he could never let her marry Fletcher now. If she was going to fall back to her old love for his cousin, Simon was going to have to stop it. He would have her, one way or the other.

He turned away while Zach and the Scofields walked to the hotel. On the steps of the large white building, Zach was grim as he looked around.

"Well, I can't arrest him. He ain't wanted. And he ain't done nothin'. And he's going to be charmin' all the ladies, that's for sure."

"He's just bidin' his time," Levi growled.

Sally sat down on the bench in front of the hotel, too exhausted to stand. Levi paused as Luke supported him. The rancher had no color and looked ready to collapse.

"Sally, honey, come on in to bed."

"I want to talk to Zach."

"You get her inside safely, will you, Zach?" "Yes."

Levi hesitated. "Sally, honey, don't listen to that Fletcher Dannack's fancy talk."

"But what if it's true? What if the witness did lie?" Her father shrugged. "I heard the witness changed his story and lied on the stand to get Dannack off, but I'll write some letters and find out. But until we know for sure, you stay away from him. If he's lyin', he's a dangerous man."

Luke helped his father inside, and Zach came to stand near Sally in the light of the lantern hung near the entrance. She was sitting with her arms folded, her head down. She looked up when she heard Zach approach.

"Zach, tell me what you think. Is Fletcher lying?"

"Yes."

"But how can you be sure?"

"I've been a lawman a long time, Sally."

Tears trickled down her face. "But I'm not sure, Zach."

"Are you still in love with him?"

She had a hard time answering. Finally, she shook her head. "I don't know. So much came back to me when I saw him."

"Your father's plenty worried."

"He's very protective, but if Fletcher is innocent, and we have no proof that he's not, we have to give him a chance."

"Why?"

Slowly, she stood up, her hand to her face. "Zach, what shall I do?"

"Stay away from him."

"And if I don't?"

"I'll blow his head off."

"What?"

He grinned, and she had to smile, relieved that the tension was broken. She moved closer, putting her hand on his arm. He stiffened, wanting to reach for her.

In a moment, she would be in his arms. He felt his blood racing, his heart drumming, his every muscle prepared to draw her into his embrace. Her eyes glistened in the starlight, and her lips were parted as she moved toward him.

Zach opened his arms and drew her against him, encircling her tightly. Her lips were inches from his, and she slid her hands up to his shoulders, her fingers digging into his shirt.

Zach was about to kiss her when Luke appeared in the doorway. "Sally, Pa's worried about you."

Sally didn't answer or turn her head. Zach ignored her brother. Something warm and wonderful was passing between him and Sally, and he wasn't about to let her go. Her breath was cool on his face.

Zach bent his head. His lips captured hers. She tasted sweet and fresh. Her body was soft in his arms. He was bursting with pleasure as he kissed her continually. She kissed him back, holding him tight.

Then slowly she drew back, and he released her. She gazed at him a long moment, his hands on her arms, and then she smiled with a softness in her eyes.

Luke was staring. She didn't look at her brother as she went inside the hotel, but she glanced over her shoulder at Zach, and she was still smiling.

Both men watched her go to the stairs, then they looked at each other. Luke was still amazed.

"I thought she was just flirting with you."

Zach grinned. "Maybe she is."

"Does this mean I don't have to worry about you and Emily?"

"Maybe."

"I wouldn't mind one bit if Sally married you, Zach. You're a decent man as I see it. But you don't have a clear field with her, you know. There's still Simon. And Dannack ain't gonna give up."

"I know that."

"When a man's crazy about a woman, there ain't much he wouldn't do."

"Are you talkin' about Emily?"

Luke grunted and went back inside, leaving Zach to wonder about the extent of Luke's involvement in Ricky's death. He liked Luke, and it would pain him, but he had been disappointed by other men in his life as a lawman, so he would never be surprised.

Emily was a lovely woman who knew how to manipulate men with her charms. She had led Zach on for months, and all the while, she had been planning to marry his brother. Perhaps even now, she was not being honest with Luke or Tealman.

While Zach thought about her, Emily was sitting on the bench on the porch of the boardinghouse. Ray Tealman sat with her, his arm about her to keep her warm.

The moon was rising, casting soft light upon them.

"Listen to me, Emily. It's time we got married. I'm courtin' you in the open like you wanted. We're doin' everything proper."

"I don't even know if I want to stay in Reata."

"Look, I've fixed up the house for you. Even brought that rosewood piano all the way from St. Louis."

She glanced around at passersby. "So much has happened, Ray. And now Luke has asked me to marry him."

"You're in love with me, not Luke Scofield." "I'm just confused, Ray."

"Confused because the Scofield spread is a hundred times the size of what I got? And because old man Scofield has a lot of money in the bank?"

His hand gripped hers so tight she winced.

"Listen to me, Emily. Do you think Luke Scofield would marry you if he knew everything?"

TEN

On Sunday morning, the good citizens of Reata went to church. The ladies were in their finery, and the gents wore their Sunday best. It was warm and clear, with no breeze.

At the hotel, Zach was dozing in the lobby when Sally came down the stairs with Luke holding her arm. Zach stood up, removing his hat and running his hand over his curly black hair, feeling in need of a bath. "Good morning," he said, a bit awkwardly.

Sally was wearing a green silk dress with lace at the collar. She was pale, her eyes red from lack of sleep. "Zach, did you spend the night here?"

"I sort of fell asleep."

She smiled, her eyes flashing. "You spent the night here because of me."

Zach forced a frown. "Why would I do that?"

A soft laugh came from her rosy lips. "Because you're a very foolish but very honorable man."

"I reckon I just don't trust Fletcher Dannack." She sobered. "I'm sure everything will be all right, Zach. And it's very possible he's telling the truth."

"I'd say a chance in ten thousand."

Luke nodded. "Listen to him, Sally."

"But Father always said we should be fair to others. They pardoned Fletcher, and we owe him at least to be civil."

"You cornin' to church?" Luke asked Zach.

"I need to freshen up. I'll join you later."

Sally smiled and nodded, and she walked out with Luke. Zach stood at the entrance, watching the parade of people grimly. Among them strolled Fletcher Dannack, escorting two elderly ladies and charming them easily.

Dannack was smart, all right. He was taking it slow. Zach went upstairs to where Levi was resting, and he pulled up a chair by the bed. "You look ready to ride."

Levi grunted. "I'm stiff and sore, but I'm healing. The doc is sure fussin' over me. Said I got up too soon. But he forgets how many times he's patched me up over the years. You goin' to church?"

"As soon as I get me a bath."

"I'm worried, Zach. I mean, terrible worried. Dannack is going to win the town over before he makes his move. I can't figure his game, except to marry Sally and get the ranch. He plays the game long enough, he might convince her he was innocent the whole time."

"I hope you're wrong."

"By the way, Luke came up here last night and told me he saw you and Sally kissing, and she liked it fine. What's going on between you two?"

"If I knew, I'd tell you, Levi. But she's the brightest, most playful, gentlest female I've ever met. It's a pleasure just talking to her. Not to mention she's the most beautiful woman I've ever seen."

"That's a mouthful."

"You're her father. You have a right to know what I'm thinkin'."

"I still don't."

Zach grinned. "Maybe it depends somewhat on what you're thinkin'."

"Then I'll tell you. Simon Oliver is a fine, outstanding man with culture and education, and he'd be a fine husband for any young woman."

"But?"

Levi grinned. "You got me figured right, Zach. You're a lot like me, you know. A tough hombre. And it'd take a man like you to look after a girl like Sally. If I had my druthers, it'd be you, not Simon. But you and me, we ain't never gonna be able to tell Sally what to do."

Zach chuckled. "No, but it's sure fun trying."

Zach left the rancher and had a good hot bath, donned a clean shirt under his vest, and headed for church. By the time he got there, the congregation was singing.

Inside, Zach saw Sally sitting between Simon and Luke to his right, Jed Long in a row behind her. To his left but a few rows forward, Fletcher Dannack was busy impressing the ladies. Emily was sitting with Ray Teal man in the front row.

Zach slid into a back seat and joined in the singing, but he could hear Sally's sweet, clear soprano rising above the others.

"Amazing Grace, how sweet the sound,
That saved a wretch like me,

I once was lost but now I'm found,
Was blind, but now I see."

Zach fell silent, listening to the hymn and the way her voice spread through him like the soft glittering of starlight.

But as he listened, he thought back to Lock's Ferry and the terrible news in the paper. He recalled the frantic ride south and how he had learned nothing on arrival. Visiting his brother's grave had been painful and haunting.

His main purpose here was to avenge his brother. He still didn't know if Levi Scofield had arranged to have Ricky lynched. Levi was used to being in charge, to being powerful, and yet he would have had to have some reason other than rustling to hang a gunsmith.

Both Ray Tealman and Luke were crazy in love with Emily. Either one of them could have wanted her husband out of the way. And either one could have been with her that night.

As the service ended, Fletcher Dannack stood up and graciously helped two elderly ladies to their feet, then escorted them forward. He bowed toward Sally and smiled, then exited. As Zach went outside, he saw Fletcher politely walking the elderly women down to the boardwalk and uptown. Jed followed at a distance.

Luke came forward in the crowd with Sally on his arm, and he looked angry. "He's sure playin' it cool." Zach nodded. "He's settin' us up. Watch yourself." Pausing, Zach looked at the worried smile on Sally's face. Zach wanted to reach out and hold her hand. Instead, he teased her.

"I'll be claimin' my prize right soon."

She made a face. "We'll see about that."

"We have a bargain, remember? If you had won, I would have paid you five dollars, right? But my prize, well, when I get around to collecting, it'll be worth a lot more."

"You mean in money?" she asked.

"It's not money I'm after."

She lifted her chin. "Zach Lassiter, you can name your prize, but we'11 just have to see whether you claim it or not."

Luke stared back and forth between them. "Sally, what are you talking about?"

Sally laughed, eyes twinkling. She turned to walk down the slope with her brother.

Simon Oliver came out of the church, looking very disappointed when he discovered that Sally was gone.

He noticed Zach standing some distance away, and he turned toward the church to see Emily waiting for Tealman, who had paused to talk with some of his friends.

Emily came over to Simon as he tipped his hat. They stood alone in the sunlight.

"Good morning, Mrs. Lassiter."

"Simon," she whispered.

"What is it this time?"

"Please, keep your voice down. I don't know what's going on with you and Fletcher, but please, I beg you, don't let anything happen to Luke."

"I thought it was Ray Tealman you wanted."

"I changed my mind."

"Bless your mercenary little heart."

She drew herself up. "Don't talk to me that way."

"Keep your voice down."

"I'm the one who wrote you that Sally was here, remember?

You must help me. We have to talk, Simon."

"Come to the office tomorrow."

Simon turned and walked down the slope.

Zach had paused to watch the crowd, and he hadn't missed the encounter between Emily and Simon, which made him mighty curious. He still didn't know who had arranged his brother's death. There were ranchers here with small spreads, every one of them having some kind of grudge against Antler.

He saw Tealman talking among them, and he was a man who had a reason to make Emily a widow. So was Luke.

Zach stiffened as he saw Emily walking over to him. She looked lovely, as usual, and lifted her parasol. They were alone, away from the others, and she spoke softly. "I'm glad I had a chance to talk to you, Zach." He shrugged and didn't answer.

She took his arm. "At the dance, you asked me where I was the night Ricky was killed. Your accusation upset me, Zach, but now I can tell you why no one answered the door that night."

Zach was sober, his blue eyes darkening.

"I didn't think anyone would understand, Zach. Ricky had gone off to deliver some guns, and a dutiful wife would have held supper until after midnight."

"And?"

"When I heard he was murdered, I just couldn't tell anyone I was in bed, sound asleep. I wasn't well, and I just went to bed early, that's all, and I wasn't dressed to answer the door. How could I admit I was sound asleep while Ricky was being hanged?"

"So you lied."

"Don't say it like that, Zach."

"Maybe you're still lying."

111

She released his arm, her face flushed with color. "Zach, I remember that about you. You don't trust anyone."

Ray Tealman, having seen her talking alone with Zach, came hurrying over to join them. He took Emily's arm, his face pink with jealousy.

"What do you want, Lassiter?"

"Ray, it's all right. Remember, he was Ricky's brother."

"But you knew 'em both in Kansas."

"Ray, you're hurting my arm."

"Sorry, honey. Listen, Lassiter, I plan to marry this lady, and if you get in my way, it'll be the last time."

"You'll kill me?"

"Maybe."

"Is that what you done to my brother?"

Tealman's face tightened with dark anger. "You're twistin' my words. I ain't done nothin' to your brother. A bunch of vigilantes done that."

Zach looked from the nervous Emily to Tealman, and then he turned to walk down the slope. He still didn't believe Emily. And he still didn't know who had murdered Ricky.

Back in town, Zach strolled the streets with Jed. They had seen Dannack in the Lucky Lady playing cards, with no one contacting him. They took turns sleeping and walking the town all night, but nothing happened.

While the lawmen had breakfast at the cafe on Monday morning, Fletcher Dannack put on his new white shirt and stand-up collar. He brushed his long coat and patted his clean-shaven face, his thin nose a little damp with his excitement.

He strolled down the sunny street, where activity was in full swing. Wagons, horses, mules, and a lot of people were crowding each other. Yes, this was a prosperous town.

He entered the bank and went up to the sleepy old teller. "I have a rather large deposit. I'd like to see the manager, please."

The clerk went back and knocked on Simon's door. He then escorted Fletcher into the office and closed the door behind him as he left.

Simon was seated behind his desk, fingertips together.

"Well, cousin," Fletcher said with a grin, "here we are at last."

"We got to talk."

Fletcher sat down in a leisurely fashion and removed his hat. He smoothed his sandy hair. "That's why I'm here. You see before you a free man. I got me a full pardon. With a bit of persuasion and a lot of desire to stay alive, that witness changed his mind and apologized to the court."

"Listen, Fletcher—"

"And the judge apologized to me. He even said what a fine man I appeared to be, that I was generous and forgiving."

"Fletcher—"

"So here I am. And I still have the bank money stashed away. Ready to wed Sally and her ranch."

"The deal's off."

"Wait a minute. As soon as we heard from Cousin Emily, I sent you here with a lot of my bank loot so you could set things up for me."

"That was before I met Sally."

Fletcher smiled lazily. "I see."

"I'm in love with her. I want to marry her, Fletcher."

"So do I."

"Blast it, stop taking things so easy. I'm serious." "I know you are. Well, we'll let Sally choose, shall we?"

113

"You mean that?"

"Would I lie to my cousin?"

Simon wasn't so sure, but he had a lot of respect for Fletcher's prowess with a gun and the fact that he was a cold-blooded killer, so he wasn't going to push his luck.

Fletcher pushed his hat back. "Now, how have Chips and the boys been doing?"

"They been following orders."

"But there are two Scofield men still alive. I want Sally to be the only one left. Then I'll be running Antler, and you and me, we'll both get rich. That was the plan, remember?"

Simon shrugged. "They got Leroy. Almost got Levi. But Emily wants us to lay off Luke. I thought she wanted Tealman. Now she's changed her mind and wants Luke and her share of Antler."

"Luke goes, and that's final. It's going to be me and Sally on that spread, and nobody else. You're getting paid plenty. So you go ahead and take care of Luke and the old man."

"Seems like you got to get rid of the law first."

Fletcher smiled. "What for? They look easy to me."

"Well, Jed Long's the sheriff, and he's pretty careful. But it's the deputy you got to worry about."

"The deputy. Yes, he was fast on the draw. First man ever to come close to me. But I assumed he just got lucky. Who is he?"

"Zach Lassiter."

Fletcher was surprised, then delighted. "Well, so we finally meet. I've been hearing about him for years. No wonder."

"He's no fool. We've got to get rid of him."

"What's the hurry?"

"He's sweet on Sally."

"And, I imagine, so is the rest of the town. Well, Simon, we have to do everything slow and easy. And you and me, we've got to have an alibi at all times. So where are the men?"

"Camped in the buttes at Coyote Creek, just waiting for you to show up. But I don't cotton to that Chips."

"Ah, yes. He once skinned a man alive."

Simon winced and shook his head. "Figures."

"Well, I'm going to look around for a business to start to show how respectable I am." Both men stood up and shook hands. "May the best man win, Simon." Simon watched him leave, looking grim as the door closed. Alone, he sat at his desk, fingertips together, organizing his angry thoughts, desperate to end up with Sally. He didn't like Zach hanging around, but Chips Rafferty could get rid of him. It was Fletcher he was worried about, because Sally might still be in love with him, and his cousin was silver-tongued.

Outside on the boardwalk in the morning sunlight, Fletcher Dannack strolled until he met two of the ladies from church. They invited him to their home.

Across the street, Zach witnessed this. Grim, he went to the hotel to see Levi. Sally was sitting by his bed. The rancher was dressed, without his boots, and was propped up and looking right fine.

"Hi, Zach. Doc says 1 can go home in a day or two."

"Where's Luke?"

"He went back to the ranch with some of the boys."

Not wanting to alarm Levi, Zach took the news casually and stood up. "Well, I'll ride out and have a look. Maybe the rustlers are still around."

"Nothin's happened since you got them five."

"Sally got one of 'em," Zach reminded him. "She saved my life. You know, some Indians believe if you save a life, you have to watch over it until the favor's returned."

Sally wrinkled her nose. "You want me to protect you?"

Zach grinned. "Okay with me."

"You be careful out there," Levi said.

"I will, but I want Sally to stay with you at all times."

Sally stood up, annoyed. "Fletcher is being a perfect gentleman. And I have some shopping to do."

"You'll stay with your father."

"Don't tell me what to do."

Zach grimaced. "This badge is telling you what to do."

She rose up as tall as she could. "I will do as I please and when I please."

Zach came closer to her, glaring down at her. "Fletcher Dannack is here for one reason only, and that's to get his hands on you. And I'm thinkin' he's been behind all that's happened around here."

"He was pardoned. He may well have been innocent," she insisted.

"If you won't do it for your sake, do it for your father. You should be here watching out for him. You're a fine shot, and he could use you right here. Or have you forgotten someone's trying to kill off the Scofield men?"

Sally turned pale. "All right, Zach. You win." Levi seemed amused, but he said nothing.

She walked into the hallway with Zach, closing the door behind her. "You're a stubborn man."

"Just be careful."

He wanted to reach for her, but he held back and turned to

head for the stairs, knowing he had to hurry to catch up with Luke. And besides, it wasn't proper to be kissing her in a hotel.

But Sally caught his arm, stopping him, and he turned to look down at her. They were alone on the empty landing with no one below in the lobby, and she was so fetching, he had to take a deep breath. "Zach—"

Before she could finish, he seized her by the arms and pulled her against him, holding her on her tiptoes, her lips inches from his, her dark eyes wide and gleaming.

Zach bent closer, and kissed her soundly. She was warm and soft in his embrace, and she kissed him back. Then he held her tight, her face at his chest. Suddenly, she pushed him away, and he drew back to follow her glance down into the lobby. Simon Oliver was watching them, and now he was coming up the stairs, his face dark with angry color.

"Sir, are you taking advantage of this young lady?" Zach grinned and pulled his hat down tight. He started to walk past Simon, who had reached the landing and blocked his path.

"Listen to me, Zach. I catch you annoying Miss Scofield again, and we'll have to fight it out." "Name your weapons."

"I will, when the time comes."

"You've asked her to marry you, have you?"

"That's right," Simon said.

"And did she say yes?"

"Not yet, but she will. And I can tell you this, I have a lot more to offer than some gunfighter with a badge."

"Why don't we let the lady make up her own mind?"

"She's young and impressionable. I have to protect her from men like you."

"Then do your best."

117

With a grin, Zach turned, tipped his hat to the rosy-faced Sally, and went on down the stairs. Sally's kiss was still warm on his lips, and he figured never to erase that kiss with so much as a cup of coffee.

But he was anxious to find Luke before there was trouble. Scofield men had become targets.

At the hotel entrance, Zach turned, looking back to the landing where Sally stood watching him, Simon at her side. She lifted her hand to wave, and Zach nodded. She looked lovely and flushed with color, her smile touching him.

Although he didn't know how he felt about Emily, Zach had no trouble figuring his feelings for Sally. She was just downright lovable, and every time he was near her, he fell apart with joy. Her very touch curled his toes.

Zach looked at her for a long moment, then turned.

When Zach had left the hotel, Simon turned to Sally with his hat in hand. "Sorry. When a man's in love, he loses his head. Forgive me?"

"Yes, of course, Simon."

"Zach Lassiter is a gunfighter, a lawman, a nothing. And I have so much to offer. A fine family back East. Money in the bank. An inheritance coming. And I'm well-educated and a gentleman. Spend your life with me, and you'll never be sorry."

"I'll let you know, Simon."

"Men like Lassiter leave a lot of widows behind. And Fletcher Dannack, well, I don't trust him. He's not the man you knew, Sally. He's a cold-blooded killer."

"How do you know that? He was pardoned."

"I know men."

She frowned, his words hurting her.

He took her arm, and they went to visit Levi.

And Zach, riding his new stallion, headed for the Scofield ranch, anxious to find Luke and make sure he was still alive. But he kept seeing Sally on the landing with Simon at her side. And he worried about Fletcher Dannack's intentions.

As he rode, he thought of his brother, lynched for something he had never done. He could see Emily's sweet face, remember how he had spent five years unable to look at another woman. Now there were questions about her loyalty to his brother.

His life had gotten mighty complicated.

He was far into the Scofield ranch and its rolling hills when he heard the shots.

ELEVEN

Zach dug in his heels, and his stallion sailed over the sea of grass. The sound of gunfire was louder as he neared the narrow creek that cut through the low bluffs.

He reined up on a rise and saw Luke's horse trailing its reins. A man was in the brush by the creek, and three others were behind rocks on the opposite side, taking potshots at him.

Zach had no way to get around the three attackers without being seen. His best bet was to take cover. He left his stallion behind some brush and slipped through the rocks down toward the creek.

He made it to cover without being seen and lifted his Winchester. He knelt behind the rocks, watching.

He saw a hat at the highest rock across the creek, and he fired. There was a yell and a crashing sound. Suddenly, gunfire opened up on Zach. He could see a man running along the bluff, probably heading for his horse, and Zach fired, cutting him down. The third man was firing rapidly, missing both Zach and Luke, and then there was silence.

The man was reloading. Zach leaped from the rocks and went

running across the shallow water, splattering it in all directions, charging up the slope.

But he was too late. The man raised up with a rifle and aimed dead center at Zach. Hitting the dirt, Zach rolled and fired, his bullet slamming into the man's chest. The man gasped, then fell over.

Zach got to his feet. He saw Luke rising from the brush, but he waved him back. He went up the slope to find all three men dead, and signaled Luke to come over. But Luke didn't move. Zach crossed the creek and headed for the brush, where he found Luke crumpled up and looking desperate.

Luke had been creased on the side of his head, blood trickling down his neck. His shirt was torn from the brush. He looked stunned, waving his six-gun at Zach until he could see him clearly.

"I'm sure glad to see you, Zach. They shot me clean out of the saddle. I rolled down here, and when I hit the brush, my head felt like it had been slammed with a rock. Then all of a sudden, I couldn't see nothin'. But it's comin' back now."

"There was three of 'em. All dead now."

"I'll take a look. See if I know 'em."

Zach helped Luke to stand up and lean on him, and they crossed over the creek. Luke looked long and hard at each of the three men.

"Don't know 'em, Zach. They got any papers on 'em?"

Zach let Luke sit down on a rock, and he searched the men. "Not a sign. You rest while I look at their horses."

But the horses had various brands from Arizona and Kansas. He brought the animals down to where Luke was waiting. Luke had tied his bandanna around his head.

"Whoever figured this out," Zach said, "he was pretty smart, makin' sure nothin's traced to 'im."

At the ranch, Primo and two of the men were outside the corrals and hurriedly came to meet them. Primo cast ugly glances at Zach, but he helped Luke down from the saddle.

Oscar Wallace came hurrying out of the bunkhouse to hear the story, and he was fretting.

"Luke, I ain't lettin' you out of my sight."

"Fine with me," Luke said. "You can bunk at the house until Levi and Sally come back."

Oscar and Zach fussed over him all evening.

The next morning, while Oscar was making flapjacks out at the ranchhouse, Fletcher Dannack was charming the town of Reata. He talked to several merchants who might want to sell their stores. He spoke with nice little elderly ladies, bowing and kissing their hands.

But when he ran into Jed, he met a cold, clear gaze.

Fletcher was walking with two merchants and an elderly woman when Jed confronted him. "You ain't foolin' anyone, Dannack. We all know your real name is Hickman. How you got that pardon, I'll never know. But I ain't lettin' you swindle anyone in this town." Fletcher's face went pale, but his eyes narrowed. The people with him were stunned, and one of the merchants wiped his brow.

"Hickman? You're Fletcher Hickman?"

"I was proven innocent," Fletcher growled. Quickly, the merchants took the lady away and headed down the street, murmuring. Soon the town would be whispering about the charming man from Missouri who was really an ex-convict, a man accused of murder and bank robbery.

Fletcher's face turned red with fury. "What kind of game are you playing, Sheriff?"

"I'm telling you straight. You ain't welcome in Reata."

"You just signed your death warrant."

Fletcher spun and went into the Lucky Lady, while Jed drew a deep breath and crossed over to the hotel, where Levi and Sally were now sitting on a bench in the shade.

"Well, I just blew his cover."

Levi nodded. "I could tell."

"Maybe it wasn't fair," Sally said.

"I couldn't let him take over this town," Jed told them. "Now the word will get around, and he won't be trusted."

Sally frowned. "But what if he was innocent?"

"Just like a woman," Levi said. "You worry over lost fawns and eagles with broken wings, and you fret and cry over everything you read in the newspaper, and that's why you need a man around when it comes to trouble."

She stiffened, chin up. "Father, that's so old-fashioned."

"You figure you can handle this Fletcher Dannack thing all by yourself?"

"No," she said, looking unhappy.

It was late that afternoon, when he was riding through the hills and along the creek heading for town, that Zach began to sense trouble. Yet there was no sign of anyone, and he convinced himself he was being too careful.

As he rode along beside the shining water, he thought of the days he and his brother had spent hunting and fishing in the mountains when they were young, long before Zach had taken up the badge. There had been no Emily. Only green mountains and valleys and crystal streams. They had laughed and fought and shared their dreams.

Now Ricky was dead. And his widow was acting suspicious.

Zach had learned nothing of his death. Instead, he was caught up in someone else's war. Scofields were being murdered. But somehow, somewhere, he sensed it was all connected.

A shot rang out. The bullet whistled by Zach's neck, slicing his bandanna. He spun the stallion and headed for the shelter of the bank on the far side, even as bullets crashed by his head. Suddenly one struck him in the back, high and near the left shoulder, in almost the same spot where he had been creased, hitting hard and brutal, nearly knocking him from the saddle.

At the rocks at the foot of the high bank, he fell to the ground and rolled behind a large stone, where he could pretend death and yet peer out. Whoever had been shooting was on the bank above him, but he was so far in, they would not be able to see him without exposing themselves.

He lay still, but his shoulder hurt like blazes.

The stallion stood nearby, nosing his boot.

Six-gun in hand, Zach waited. He could hear his heart pounding in his chest. His blood was hot and fiery in his veins. Sweat covered his face and body as the shock left him and the pain was suddenly severe.

The stallion's head rose up and turned. Zach tensed and moved for a better view.

A stocky man was coming down the bank in a hurry, rifle in hand. Now he was coming around the rock.

Zach lay still, his eyes but slits, pretending death.

"Well, that's the end of you, Lassiter."

It was Primo, standing over him and laughing. Zach wasn't inclined to kill him, and waited for him to leave. But Primo wasn't finished. He was chuckling.

"That badge didn't do you no good, Lassiter. But I'm gonna be nice to you. I'll finish you off so you won't even know the buzzards are here. Maybe I'll even get paid for it."

Primo's lifted rifle cast a shadow.

Zach had no choice. He rolled aside as the bullet spit the dirt. He raised his six-gun and fired point-blank, hitting the startled Primo right between the eyes.

The gunman staggered backward, his eyes bugging. He tried to raise the rifle, tried to work the lever. And he died on his feet, keeling over backward, then falling into the water with a splash.

Zach rose up slowly and headed for Rocket. He was hurting above the collarbone, and he was plumb tired of being shot at, but he was going to get on that stallion, one way or another.

Holstering his six-gun, he grabbed the stirrup and began pulling himself up. It was a long, painful time before he was sliding onto the saddle.

It was dark when he reached town, riding into the street where lanterns marked some of the store entrances and cast eerie lights in the dust. He made it to the livery, where a startled Ryan took the reins and led him over to the sheriff's office, then pounded on the door.

Jed came out, startled.

"Zach, not again."

Ryan helped lower Zach and walk him into the office. Then he promised to send the doctor and take care of Rocket.

Zach stretched out on his cot. "Hurts like sin."

Jed pulled up a chair and started pulling off Zach's leather vest. "Got you on the shoulder, did he? Same place as before. See who it was?"

"Primo."

"Did you get him?"

"Right between the eyes."

Jed nodded and set about peeling Zach's bloody shirt off the shoulder. Zach told him about the attack on Luke.

"Oscar's going to watch out for Luke now. And they're coming to town tomorrow with some of their men to take Levi and Sally home."

The doctor arrived, and while he worked on Zach, Jed went to tell Levi his son had been attacked but was all right.

While Zach rested, Simon Oliver had Fletcher Dannack as a guest in his plush, velvet-trimmed parlor. He had been drinking whiskey for an hour with his cousin, but it hadn't dulled his anger and frustration. He knew that if he didn't stop Fletcher, the man would either marry Sally or take her away.

Lamplight cast strange shadows on Fletcher's face as he wiped his mouth with his lace-trimmed handkerchief. "I've got to get Sally alone. I have to talk to her."

"What makes you think she'll marry you?"

"She was in love with me back in Missouri, and she can't forget that easily. I can still see it in her eyes."

"What if Levi won't let her?"

"You mean if we fail to get rid of him? Then she'll run away with me. We'll have children, and before you know it, she'll be writing her father how happy she is, and what a fine man I am, and he'll invite us back. One way or another, I'll have my share of Antler."

"And what about Luke?"

"He has to go."

"And me?"

"You're set up here, Simon. You got a nice house. You can have any woman in town."

"It's Sally I want."

Fletcher laughed. "Now Simon, you know I could kill you at the drop of a hat, so just sit back and do as I tell you. When I marry Sally, you'll have to back off."

"I can't let you do it."

"And why not?"

"Because you're a cold-blooded killer."

"It depends on how you look at it," Fletcher said. "That bank teller shot at me first, you know. And what makes you so innocent? You've been paying men to kill her brothers and father."

"That was your idea."

Fletcher smiled and sipped his whiskey. "Chips and his men would testify you're the one that hired them to rustle Antler cattle and do the killings."

"I don't care. I can't let you marry her."

"Simon, we've had too much whiskey tonight. Now, I'm headin' for the hotel for a good night's sleep. I'll see you in the morning when your head is clear."

Simon's face was burning. He was intoxicated but rational, yet out of control. He watched Fletcher stand up and start for the door. Fury engulfed him. He thought quickly how Sally would love him once Fletcher was gone. He could say the man had forced his way in, drunk and disorderly, admitting his guilt and looking for Sally to steal her away, and to save her, Simon had been forced to kill him.

Fletcher walked to the door, his back still turned.

"Good night, Simon."

Simon slid his hand inside his coat and pulled out his Smith & Wesson. He rose up, drew back the hammer, aimed unsteadily, and pulled the trigger.

But Fletcher had heard him move and leaped aside, and he spun around, six-gun in hand, firing. Simon's bullet missed, but Fletcher's hit Simon in the left chest, knocking the banker back onto the couch like a sack of flour. Simon's eyes were wild; blood soaked his shirt, and his revolver was still grasped in his white-knuckled hand.

Fletcher walked over, smiling down at him.

"I always was smarter than you, cousin."

Simon was gasping for breath. "Get a doctor."

"No, you just lie there and die. Maybe they'll find you tomorrow. I suppose they'll think someone tried to rob you."

"You can't—"

And Simon choked on his own blood. He stared at Fletcher as his cousin turned the lamp down so that the flame was gone. In the pitch dark of the room, Fletcher went back to the door, opening it and peering out.

He was certain the town had heard the shots, but no one would come looking at a dark house, at least not right away. He saw no one. He slipped out and closed the door, and walked quickly through the next alley, hurrying down the back way to the hotel.

TWELVE

Zach was sleeping in the jail and Jed was at his desk when they heard the muffled shots. Zach sat up on his cot, his shoulder aching. It took several moments for them to decide which direction the shots had come from.

"I'll take a look," Zach said.

"You've just been patched up. I'll go."

"We'll both go, and spread out."

Jed stood up, six-gun in hand, and walked in the moonlight, carefully moving uphill through the houses, listening and watching. Zach moved through the alleys nearby, his shoulder still aching. It was cold, and the air was still.

Another shot barked in the night, echoing. It came from Simon's house. Zach walked faster, keeping in the shadows as much as possible, and then he saw the white house with the roses in front. He reached the front steps at the same time as Jed.

Simon was lying in the doorway, face down, where he had crawled, gun in hand, having fired to get attention and bring help. Jed knelt, turning the man on his side. Simon Oliver was alive but unconscious, blood all over his shirt.

"Hang on, Simon," Jed murmured. "We'll get you to the doc."

Zach looked through the house quickly, while Jed skirted the area. There was no sign of anyone, and it was obvious that whoever had done the shooting had long ago vanished.

The two lawmen made a chair with their arms and lifted the unconscious man, carrying him downhill as fast as they could.

The doctor received them quickly. He worked on Simon, but kept shaking his head. "I'm not sure he'll make it, and it's not likely he'll ever wake up. I'd say he's in a coma."

Back outside in the moonlight, Zach wearily sat on the bench in front of the doctor's office. Jed stood nearby and leaned on a post.

"Now what?" Zach grumbled. "First my brother is murdered, and I'm pretty much convinced it was to get Emily. Then Leroy's killed, and they try to get Levi and Luke, and that's got to be Fletcher's way of gettin' Sally and the ranch. Now Simon's been shot. And I figure there's some connection. But we can't prove nothin'."

"And why was Simon shot?"

Zach leaned back. "That's what's got me puzzled."

The next day, Simon was still unconscious. When Sally learned of his shooting, she came to visit, with

Jed and Zach watching. The banker was lying on a table with the doctor still fussing over the bandages.

Sally had tears in her eyes, and she touched Simon's hand, but it remained limp even as she spoke. "Oh, Simon, who would do this to you?"

Outside with Zach and the sheriff in the warm sunlight, Sally touched her eyes with her lace handkerchief. "He's a nice man, Zach. Why would someone shoot him? Was it a robbery?"

"We don't know."

"We're going back to the ranch today. Will you come?" she asked.

"Later. In a few days, maybe. Oscar's bringing Luke and enough men to get you home safely."

The doctor came outside, wiping his face.

It was then that they noticed Fletcher Dannack coming along the boardwalk. He was well-dressed, as usual, and removed his hat as he smiled at Sally. "You're up early, Miss Sally."

"Haven't you heard?" she asked. "Simon Oliver was shot."

"Who, that banker fellow?"

"Yes. Did you know him?"

"Just to make my rather large deposits. Is he dead?"

"He's dying," she said. "He was unconscious when they found him, and he hasn't come to. We may never know what happened."

The doctor nodded wearily. "He'll be gone any minute." Then he went back inside, closing the door behind him, while Fletcher looked as if he really cared. "I'm sorry, Sally. You must have liked him."

She dabbed at her eyes again. Fletcher ignored the glares of the two lawmen and came a little closer. "Sally, we haven't had time to talk."

"About what?"

"About you and me, Sally."

"There is no you and me, Fletcher."

"Can't we talk by ourselves? You owe me that." She hesitated, then nodded and turned to the lawmen. "It's all right. He can walk me to the hotel." Zach was furious but didn't move. "He ain't goin' inside with you."

"No," she said.

Fletcher offered his arm, but she didn't take it. Walking with him along the boardwalk, she kept glancing at him and his big smile. She remembered her happiness so long ago when they had been planning a wedding. At eighteen, she had been so in love and so impressed with this man. Some of the warmth still remained.

"Fletcher, when I saw you at the shooting match, I was so startled, I didn't know how to react."

"I know."

"I realize your pardon means you were innocent."

"Yes. It was a full, unconditional pardon."

"And I remember how it was with us, back in Missouri. But I realize now that it was a century ago."

"Sally, don't—"

"Fletcher, I don't want to hurt you, but when I awakened this morning, I lay there a long while remembering and trying to understand, and finally I knew why I was so confused. Nothing's the same anymore. Not me, not you, and not the world in which we live."

"But you can't reason away emotions."

"I'm sorry, Fletcher. I just don't love you anymore."

He was grim, hands into fists. "So who do you love? That fancy banker?"

"I don't know."

"Or that gunfighter?"

She stopped in front of the hotel and turned to gaze up at him. "Fletcher, all I know for certain is that I don't love you. Perhaps I never did. I was young and very impressed with you."

"Sally, if you'll let me call on you, things will go back to the way they were with us. I promise."

"No, Fletcher. First, my father would never allow it, and second, I've already told you. There's nothing between us and there never will be."

"If we could just see each other, I know you would change your mind. Just being with me, holding hands, taking long walks, sitting in the moonlight and talking the way we used to, just the two of us, you'd love me again."

"I'm sorry, Fletcher."

She rose on her tiptoes and put her hand on his arm.

She kissed his cheek and drew back with a smile. He was staring at her as she turned away and went into the hotel.

Fletcher was beside himself with rage. He had come here to do the decent thing, court her properly, beg her to marry him, and he had failed. She was leaving him no other option.

He turned and kicked the post of the hitching rail, twice. He took off his hat and slammed his fist into it, then jerked it back on his head. Grimly, he walked across the street to the Lucky Lady while the lawmen watched. Zach pushed his hat back with relief.

"Well, he didn't get anywhere."

"Wonder what he's up to?" Jed grunted.

"I don't know, but we'd better stick with Simon. If he comes to, he might have somethin' real interestin' to tell us. And someone might want him dead in a hurry."

"I'll stay with him. You keep an eye on Fletcher Dannack."

Early in the afternoon, when Zach went into the Lucky Lady, he felt tense and apprehensive. It was something about the way Fletcher Dannack was leaning on the bar, guzzling his whiskey and letting his fancy manners give way to ugliness.

Zach looked around the saloon. There was a drunk asleep at a table in the corner. A boy of about ten was sitting on the floor near the back entrance, polishing a brass spittoon. The bartender was wiping glasses and putting them on a shelf in front of the big mirror.

Three men in trail clothes were playing cards at a table near the front window. No one was at the piano. There was a deep, brooding silence.

Zach moved to the bar some ten feet from Fletcher, who slowly turned to look at him through searing eyes. "What do you want, Lassiter?"

"I was thinking maybe you'd worn out your welcome."

Fletcher sneered and downed his whiskey, then poured another glass. "I just spent four years in love with that woman, and I'm not letting them go to waste. I don't care what you think."

"If you get drunk, you'll be sleeping it off in jail."

"I never get intoxicated, Lassiter. Educated men know how to handle their liquor. You're the one who needs some lessons."

Zach pushed his hat back with his left hand.

"I'm not worried about you, Dannack."

"That shooting match. You just got lucky."

"Maybe."

Fletcher pushed away from the bar, and his hands dropped to his sides as he pushed his coat back around his six-gun. He stood with his feet apart, his thin face twisted. He didn't look like a scholar just now. Instead, he was the image of a killer, his dark eyes narrowed and mouth curved sideways.

Zach wasn't sure he could best this man, but he wasn't backing off, even as sweat formed all over his body. He thought maybe he could talk the man down.

"You're making a mistake," Zach said.

"Listen to me, Lassiter. There's no man in this country can outdraw Fletcher Dannack. I can put three holes in you before you clear leather."

The boy with the spittoon dropped it and ran behind the bar, where he pressed close to the chubby, wide-eyed bartender. The men at the table stopped their cards, but they were out of the line of fire and didn't move.

The spittoon rolled across the floor, end to end, noisy and flopping crazily. When it hit the first table with a clatter, Fletcher reached for his Colt with lightning speed.

But he stood with his six-gun half out of the holster, frozen on the spot, for he was staring at the barrel of Zach's Army Colt, already aimed and ready.

Fletcher was stunned, so amazed that his mouth fell open. He let his six-gun slide back into the holster. His face was pale, then pink, his eyes like narrow slits in his anger. He had lost his girl, and now his pride in his fast draw had been shattered.

Furious, mouth working, Fletcher turned and put both hands on the bar. He drew a deep, angry breath, then poured himself another drink.

Zach slowly holstered his six-gun. "Now there's no reason for you to stick around, Dannack. No reason at all."

The man didn't answer, and the men at the table drew a sigh of relief. The bartender wiped his brow, and all were silent but the boy.

"Wow. The fastest gun in the West."

That made Fletcher even more furious, but he remained silent and downed his whiskey.

Zach backed away to the door, then walked outside and away from the entrance. He realized now how tense he had been.

There was no denying how fast Fletcher Dannack was, and Zach had been lucky, but maybe it would clear the air. Maybe Dannack would ride out and never come back. But Zach didn't believe that.

Later that afternoon, Oscar and Luke and nine men rode in, with a buggy for Levi and Sally. Zach was worried, but he had to believe that her family and all those hands would be enough to protect her. She looked right lovely in the sunlight, her hair gleaming like red satin.

Zach helped her into the buggy, and she smiled.

"Let us know how Simon is," she told him.

Watching her fade out of his sight, Zach wished he were going with her, but Simon Oliver was still alive, and he and Jed planned to keep him that way.

In front of the doctor's office that night, Zach and Jed speculated.

"It's got to be connected," Zach said. "First Leroy, then they try to get Levi and Luke. Now Simon."

"But what connection could he have?"

"Simon wanted Sally, didn't he?"

"And who would want him out of the way?"

"Who do you think?" Zach grunted.

"Fletcher Dannack."

During the night, the lawmen took turns in the doctor's office, but no one tried to finish the job.

The next morning, clouds had filled the sky, and over at the boardinghouse, Emily was pacing in her room. She knew she could marry Luke anytime she wanted and have her share of

Antler. The problem was getting rid of Ray Tealman. If Zach could be suddenly angered, she believed he would shoot the man down.

Taking pen in hand, she wrote a few words to Zach: *If you want to know who killed Ricky, meet me at the cafe, now.*

Just before Ray Tealman called to take her to supper, she sent the note with a neighbor's young son. At the cafe, she held Tealman's hand and smiled often. He was delirious with happiness. They were all alone in the big room, and she was being quite affectionate. "So what are you saying, Emily?"

"That I'm deeply fond of you."

He squeezed her hand. "So we can name the date?" She glanced toward the door. There was no sign of Zach. She was anxious, having trouble concentrating on Tealman's words, but his question rang in her ears, and he was persistent.

"When can we set the date, Emily?"

"Tomorrow," she said.

"So, it was all worth it."

It was then that Zach came through the door. He headed for their table. Tealman glared at him. Zach ignored him and held out the note Emily had sent to him.

"What does this mean?"

Slowly, she stood up and backed away from the table. "Zach, I just learned that Ray hired some men to murder my husband."

Startled, Tealman stood up, face reddening in amazement, his mouth wide open. "It's a lie."

Zach didn't trust her. "Who told you?"

"Ray told me."

"I never said any such thing," Tealman growled. "What are you trying to pull?"

Zach felt sweat trickling down his back. Any moment, he might be forced to kill a man who could be innocent. Yet it had to be Luke or Tealman, both desperate to marry Emily.

Her face was pale. "Zach, I'm telling you the truth."

"Why didn't you tell me before?"

"I was afraid of Ray."

"You want me to believe you? Then tell me where you were the night Ricky was killed."

"I was home."

"Alone?"

"No," Tealman growled. "I was there."

Zach's face was burning. So Tealman had been with her that night while Ricky was being murdered. He turned to the rancher. For a long moment, he hated this man, and then his fury cooled as he saw the agony in the man's face.

"How'd you know my brother wasn't coming home?"

"She told me."

Zach turned to look at the shaken Emily, the woman he had loved so long ago, the woman his brother had married.

"Is that right, Emily?"

She put her hands to her face. "No, he's lying."

Tealman moved around the table. "Listen to me, Lassiter. I love this woman. But she's trying to get me killed so she can marry Luke Scofield and his ranch. Seems like my spread ain't big enough. And the name Tealman don't cut any ice like Scofield does."

Zach turned to Emily. "How did you know Ricky wasn't coming home?"

"I didn't. Ray is lying."

"But you turned down the lamps. Even if you went to sleep,

you would have left at least one lamp burning at the door. You must have known he wasn't coming home."

Emily folded her arms. "He often stayed on the ranches at night. I just believed he wasn't coming home that evening. That's all."

"She's lying," Ray said. "She got me over there, and she insisted he wasn't cornin' home that night.

And she was mighty affectionate. Turned my head, all right."

"So, married to my brother, you were in this man's arms."

Tears filled her eyes. "Zach, why do you believe him and not me?"

"I'm thinkin' how you married Ricky because he would be a better provider. Then you figured Tealman was a good catch, but he wasn't enough. Now you've got your sights set on Luke and Antler, but Tealman here, he's in the way. But why is he in the way? Why not just say no and marry Luke?"

Tealman grunted. "Because I threatened to tell Luke about our being together that night while her husband was being lynched."

Emily backed away. "You're all thinking terrible things. Luke will never believe them. I'm going home. Alone."

"I haven't finished with you," Zach said.

She moved toward the door. "You leave me alone, Zach Lassiter."

"You got someone to kill Ricky," he accused.

"That's a lie. If you ever loved me like you said you did, you'll know it's a lie."

Spinning on her heel, she stormed out into the moonlight and ran across the street. Zach stared at the open doorway, his heart pounding, his hands tight at his sides. His mouth was dry as bone.

Slowly he turned to look at Ray Tealman, but the man was a disaster, his face twisted, dark eyes wet with tears as he muttered his words.

"I was crazy in love with her."

"So was I, once."

"I swear, Lassiter, I didn't have anything to do with your brother's death. All I wanted was to be with her every chance I got. I was with her that night he was hanged, all right, and we heard someone poundin' at the door, but she kept me quiet so no one would know I was there. And we met a lot of times since, at night mostly so there'd be no gossip, but it was all innocent. I respected her, treated her like a lady, and now I feel like I was kicked by a mule."

"You think she paid someone to kill Ricky?"

"No, she wouldn't know how."

"What about Luke?"

"He kept his distance until she stopped wearin' black, and as soon as she seen Luke was interested, she started puttin' me off. I reckon she saw how rich them Scofields were, and she was figurin' on gettin' her hands on it."

Zach was flustered, confused, and angry. If he had ever felt anything for Emily, it was gone now, and he felt like an empty shell that had exploded. He sat down at the table before his legs buckled. Tealman sat opposite him.

"So she was tossin' you over for Luke?" Zach asked.

"Reckon so, but I never wanted to believe it."

"So what are you going to do now?"

Tealman shrugged. "Go home. I mean, if that's all right with you."

They stood up and shook hands, and both men left the cafe, Tealman heading for the livery and Zach back over to the doctor's office, where Jed was keeping an eye on the dying Simon. Jed was on the bench outside, his arms folded, one leg crossed over the other, trying to stay awake. It was dark and cold.

As Zach arrived, the door opened and the doctor stuck his head out. "Hey, Sheriff, Simon's awake." The lawmen hurried inside. Lamps were turned up high, and Simon was gazing at them with a blank expression. His voice was hoarse and labored, his lips white. His breathing was noisy.

"Sheriff, the doc says I'm dying."

"What does he know?" Jed grunted.

"I can't feel anything. So I know he's right."

Jed moved closer. "Who shot you?"

"Fletcher Dannack."

"But why?"

"He's my cousin. I was living in Ohio most of the time he was robbing banks in Missouri. He was always sending me money to do things for him, and I bought off the witness for his second trial. And with Primo feeding me information, I paid the rustlers to pick off Antler to cover up the rest of what Fletcher wanted done."

"Like murder Leroy?"

"We paid Chips Rafferty and his gang for rustling and killing. You'll find him easy. He wears a black-and-white cowhide vest and conchos on his hat. Has a raspy voice."

"And Fletcher told 'em to kill Scofields?" Jed asked.

"Yes, but they were clumsy about it."

"So Fletcher was after Sally," Zach cut in.

"Yes, that was the whole plan. Sally and the ranch."

"Where do you fit in?" Jed asked.

"I fell in love with Sally. Wanted to marry her, but I was afraid she was still in love with Fletcher, and I had to stop him. I tried to shoot him in the back, but he was too fast for me, even then."

"Well, it was all for nothing," Zach said. "She's turned him down."

Simon, still glassy-eyed, shook his head. "He won't care. He plans to take her away and marry her, whether she wants to or not. He thinks she'll convince her father later that it's all right. Then he can come back and get his hands on Antler."

Zach's face tightened, his eyes blazing. "She's at the ranch under guard."

Blood oozed from Simon's mouth. "Nothing will stop him."

"I'm going out there right now," Zach said.

Simon slowly turned his head as blood ran down his chin and neck. "Wait."

Zach hesitated. "I've got to hurry."

"Your brother."

"What about him?"

"Chips and his men, they did the lynching."

Zach caught his breath. "Why?"

"I paid him. For Emily. She's my cousin too. She wanted to marry Ray Tealman. She paid me back when she sold the house. I even made a profit."

Zach's face was dark red. "Well, she's changed her mind. Now she wants Luke."

"I know."

Simon was choking on his blood, and the doctor shoved the lawmen toward the door. "Let him die in peace."

Jed wiped his brow. "Well, I reckon I'd better arrest Emily Lassiter. Doc, you're a witness to his confession. That's gonna stand up in court 'counta he knowed he was dyin'. And we're sure gonna get Fletcher Dannack."

Simon closed his eyes and smiled.

Zach spun on his heel and headed outside, but his search of the town led to nothing but frustration. Fletcher Dannack had disappeared after drawing his money out of the bank. There was no sign of him or his horse.

Zach felt a cold chill. He knew where Dannack had gone.

THIRTEEN

*I*t was early light with a cloudy sky when Zach reached Antler, and what he had feared had already happened. The ranch house was a crumbling shell of blackened timber, with smoke curling from a few burning embers. Three ranch hands lay on the ground around the bunkhouse. One of them was Oscar Wallace. He was still alive, lifting a hand when he saw Zach. He had been crawling from the corrals on his belly.

Zach reined up and dismounted, kneeling quickly with his canteen in hand to give Oscar a drink, then helping him sit up in the shade against the bunkhouse steps. The foreman was bleeding from his side and right shoulder and thigh, but he was coherent.

"It was Dannack and some of his men. I got hit pretty hard, and I guess they thought I was dead. I just woke up a few minutes ago."

"What happened?"

"There was rustlin' to draw us off, way up north. Luke took most of the men and went up there. Left us short-handed. Levi was at the house when they hit us.

I don't even know if he's alive."

"And Sally?"

"I don't know."

"I'll get you in the bunkhouse, but I got to leave you."

"Luke oughta be back soon."

"Rest here a minute while I check the house."

Canteen still in hand, Zach ran up the hillside to the remains of what had been a fine house. Knowing Fletcher, he was certain Sally had not died in the fire, but what about Levi?

His stomach turning into knots, Zach walked around the ruins, and saw something crawling in the brush. He drew his Colt and walked carefully, seeing a six-gun pointed at him by a grimy-looking hand.

"Levi?"

The rancher was covered with soot, his gray eyes like small round lights in his blackened face. He was crawling on his stomach, trying to hold up his six-gun.

"Levi, it's me, Zach Lassiter."

Lowering the gun, Levi coughed and gasped. Zach hurried to kneel at his side, turning him over on his back and using his bandanna to wipe the soot from his face. Then he gave him water, and the rancher coughed and spat and coughed again.

"Levi, where's Sally?"

"Dannack got her during the night. Must of stole her out her window, then set fire to the house while I was asleep. Him and three of his gang."

"Which way did they head?"

"West, toward the Rio Grande. Probably gonna cross into Arizona Territory, right into the Apaches." "What about Luke?"

"I don't know," Levi gasped, sitting up slowly. "One of the

men came ridin' in and said they was pinned down at Apache Canyon by some rustlers. Luke took most of the men, but it could have been a setup."

"Levi, I've got to go after Sally."

"I know."

"I'll get you down to the bunkhouse. Maybe you and Oscar can look after each other."

"I ain't hurt bad. Just full of smoke. It happened awful fast. I woke up with the room on fire. I was climbin' out the window when I saw Fletcher with Sally. I didn't have my gun, and I started to yell. Some fellow in a cowhide vest, he shot me in the shoulder.

I fell out the window and landed on my head, knocked myself out. Guess they thought I was dead. When I come to, I was covered with soot, and it was all I could do to get away from the fire."

"Cowhide vest? Conchos on his hat?"

"Yeah, that's him."

"Chips Rafferty. He killed my brother."

Zach helped Levi stand, and half-carried him down the hill. Oscar had managed to get to the steps of the bunkhouse, and Zach took Levi inside, then helped Oscar.

"Take some extra horses," Levi said.

"None of 'em would keep up with Rocket."

"When Luke gets back, I'll send him after you with some of the men."

All three were wondering if they would see Luke alive again, or if they would ever find Sally. Zach helped Levi pull off his blackened, scorched clothes and change into clothes belonging to his men, and he hurriedly washed their wounds.

He made up a bedroll for himself and took supplies from the cookhouse. As he mounted Rocket, he saw Levi at the doorway, leaning on the frame.

"God be with you," Levi called.

Zach nodded and turned west, his big stallion covering the open land in great strides. He found the trail quickly. There were three men riding with Fletcher Dannack and Sally. He knew one of them was Chips Rafferty.

There was no moon because of the clouds, and he feared he would lose the trail, so he made a cold camp and forced himself to sleep. He was on his way again at first light. The air was damp, and the wind was rising. Dark clouds in the sky were promising rain, and Zach worried all the more.

While Zach was riding west across the tracks of the Denver & Rio Grande, heading toward the river,

Fletcher Dannack had already crossed the Rio Grande and was leading the way into the mountains.

Fletcher still hated Zach's beating him to the draw, but he figured he had won. He had Sally, and no one would ever find them.

She rode at his side, her hands tied to the pommel, her crimson hair spilling about her face. He had thrown a blanket over her head while she was asleep and had carried her out, but he had had the decency to gather up her riding clothes and boots. He had allowed her to dress behind bushes when they had camped the night before.

She was somber, not looking at him, staring straight ahead. She had seen her father and Oscar die, and the pain was like a knife in her heart. Luke was probably already dead, having ridden into a trap. And Zach was still in town, unaware of what had happened. Simon may already have died. She felt terribly alone and lost.

Yet deep within her was a stubborn resolve to escape.

Chips Rafferty was riding behind them with two grubby-looking men who were heavily armed, their dirty, bearded faces and chewing tobacco making them not only ugly but distasteful.

Chips wore a cowhide vest, and conchos glittered on his hatband. He whistled a lot, and she refused to look back at him, nor would she look at Fletcher. She knew that Fletcher loved her and that no harm would come to her, but these men could kill him too easily. All it would take would be a bullet in the back.

Fletcher turned in the saddle. "Chips, shouldn't your men have caught up with us by now?"

"Won't be long. But I can't figure you. If the Scofield men are all dead, why are you ridin' off? Just marry the girl and take over the ranch. They can't prove nothin'."

"You let me handle this."

Sally was aware that Fletcher was busy being his old charming self, but it frightened her.

"Sally," he said, "it grieves me that your father had to die, but it wasn't intended. But I'll make it up to you. We're going to a place where you and I will be all alone for a while. It'll be like it was, just the two of us. No one will ever find us, and in time, you'll realize we belong together."

She looked away and refused to answer.

"Sooner or later," he said, "you'll realize I had nothing to do with anything else."

"You had Leroy killed."

"No, Sally. That was Simon."

She stared at him. "What?"

"Simon was my cousin, but he had a twisted mind. He was determined to marry you and get the ranch, so he hired Chips here to rustle cattle to stir things up. Then he had Leroy killed so folks would think the rustlers were cleaning house. He's the one that tried to kill your father and Luke."

Sally looked away, her face burning.

"Sally, when I got to town and learned what Simon had been doing, I didn't want anything to do with it. I went to his house to tell him I wanted you in an honorable way. He lost his head, said he was going to marry you. I started to leave and he tried to shoot me in the back, so I shot him."

She shook her head but didn't answer.

"It was Simon all along, Sally. He ruined it for me. I had no other choice but to steal you away. I didn't think anyone would die when I came for you."

Sally closed her eyes and bit her lip, her heart aching with pain. She had wept in her blankets last night, but she would not let him see her cry. He was sincere and convincing, but she didn't trust him anymore.

They rode into the rocky, wooded slopes, and by late afternoon they could see the blue mountains with white caps and dark forest. They looked cold and unfriendly.

At twilight, they camped by a little creek that was dancing downhill over the rocks. Aspen and cottonwood surrounded them, and the dark clouds were casting a mist on the land. It would rain before long, and Sally was fretting. If anyone was following, the tracks would soon be lost.

Chips Rafferty's beady eyes were always on her, and it made her very nervous. Whenever Fletcher turned his back on Chips, the man smiled as if he was thinking how easy it would be to have her for himself. That frightened her, because she knew she was safe with Fletcher, but these other men would attack her if they had the chance.

She knew she had to escape, even if they were in Apache country. If it rained, she might have a chance.

She sat down near the fire and shivered. The food was half cold, but the coffee was very hot and thick.

It was starting to rain, the fire sizzling as the men tried to keep it going. Fletcher came to put a slicker around her shoulders.

"Are you cold, Sally?"

"Yes."

He put more blankets across her lap, then knelt. "Sally, I'm so sorry about everything. Can't you just try to remember Missouri? I used to serenade you, remember? And we took long buggy rides."

"I remember."

"Don't think about anything else but how it was."

She watched him go back to the heavy coffeepot to pour them both another cup, while Chips watched with that sinister smile that sent chills racing through her.

Fletcher stood up and stretched, pot and cups in hand.

Suddenly a bullet hit the pot, knocking it from his hand. He dropped the cups and dived from the firelight, rolling and pulling his gun.

Chips darted around the fire and grabbed Sally. She fought him, but he shoved his six-gun barrel against her cheek. Frantic, she twisted and bit his gun hand, hard.

He shrieked as blood spurted. Furious, he hit her hard with his six-gun, knocking her down, even as another bullet flew and cut his ear. She collapsed and lay at his feet, unconscious, her slicker fallen aside as rain began to soak her clothing and blankets.

Chips dived for the shadows. His other two men had already backed into the trees. Fletcher moved around on his hands and knees, trying to get to Sally, then giving up and darting into the trees.

The rifle barked again. One of the grubby men gasped and fell backward into the brush with a clatter. The other one started running for the horses, and when he hit the clearing, he was shot dead center and died on his feet.

That left Chips and Fletcher moving through the trees, trying to circle the intruder.

Zach was hovering in the brush, watching and waiting, his Winchester repeater cocked and ready. Rain was falling heavily now, soaking his shirt and hat as he crouched low and waited. Not wanting to hit Sally, he had not killed Chips Rafferty when the man struck her, but Chips was going to pay for that.

Suddenly, he saw Fletcher rise up and fire.

The bullet singed Zach's ear, and he rolled aside, firing back. Fletcher gasped, firing again, then dropping to his knees. Frantic, the man lifted his six-gun and pulled back the hammer with bloody hands. Before he could fire, Zach shot him in the middle of his chest.

Fletcher cried out and fell back, rain washing the blood away. He tried to stay upright, his eyes wild, fury keeping him alive a moment longer. Then he fell on his side and rolled over with a moan.

Zach spun at the sound of brush crackling.

Chips was taking aim, and both men fired at the same time.

Chips rose up crazily, firing again. Zach was hit in the left arm above the elbow, and he fired back.

Chips went down in the brush, but Zach could hear him crawling around. Zach dropped to his belly and moved slowly out of the line of fire, but he was making noise. The rain was pounding both of them, and he couldn't see in the heavy darkness.

Lightning flashed in the distance but gave no light here in the trees. Thunder boomed and rolled in the dark sky. The rain was beating them down, flooding them and chilling them as they fought to see each other.

"Chips Rafferty, you hanged my brother," he shouted. "I'm taking you in alive so I can see *you* hang."

There was silence. Zach had given away his position for nothing. Chips wasn't taking the bait, and he could be closing in for the kill. Despite the pouring rain, Zach was sweating under his soaked clothes. He felt needles running all over his skin. Any moment, he could die, leaving Sally with that animal.

And then Zach smelled something.

That cowhide vest, wet and stinking. Right behind him.

Zach rolled over fast and fired as Chips rose up like some wild grizzly out of the brush and fired at the same time. Zach's shot hit him square in the chest, while Chips's bullet tore through Zach's bandanna, barely missing his throat.

Chips cried out, staggered backward, twisted crazily, and then fell in a heap in the brush, firing as he died.

Zach struggled to his feet and stared down at him.

That was for Ricky, he thought, the pain of his brother's death easing for the first time, but there were tears in his eyes.

He walked over to where Fletcher lay in the pouring rain,

and knelt, shaking him. The man opened his eyes and stared at Zach in disbelief. Then he died.

Zach stood up slowly as he balanced his rifle. There was no telling when the other outlaws would show up from their fight with Luke. And worse, this was Apache country. He had to get Sally away from here.

He hurried to the campfire, which had been nearly put out by the rain, and he saw Sally lying there as if she were dead.

Frantic, Zach knelt and lifted her against him.

"Sally?"

Her head rolled back against his arm, and she gazed at him, barely conscious. There was blood on the side of her head where Chips had struck her. She tried to speak, but couldn't. Using the rain, he washed off the blood and wrapped his bandanna around her head, knotting it.

He drew the slicker around her, then lifted her in his arms, her head rolling against his chest. He was unmindful of his own wound, knowing only that he had to get her out of there. Now she was unconscious, limp in his grasp.

Fearful that she was going to die, he whispered a desperate prayer for help as rain poured down her face. She looked so pale. He kept praying.

He carried her down to the gully where Rocket was waiting. He set her on the saddle and swung up behind her, cradling her in his arms. He spun the stallion and headed east through the rough terrain.

The rain might protect them from Apaches, but it was soaking him through, and it made the trail treacherous as they headed downhill.

It was just before daylight when the rain stopped. Rocket

was carefully finding the trail down through the slippery mud. The dark sky was opening for a spray of sunlight.

And there was a rainbow, bright colors circling the sky and pointing toward home.

Sally moaned, and then discovered she was on a horse in a man's arms. She became terrified and began to struggle, fighting his grasp.

"Sally, it's me, Zach."

She twisted to gaze up at him with blurred vision, and then she focused. Relief crossed her face, and she smiled, her hand touching the bandanna. Her pain was reflected in her wince. His arms tightened around her.

Leaning back in the comfort of him, she whispered. "Zach, they killed my father, and Oscar too."

"No, they didn't. They're both alive."

She turned, joy flushing color in her face as she stared at him. "Thank God. And Luke?"

"I don't know."

Resting against him once more, she stared at the glorious rainbow. Then she turned and pressed her face to his chest. She saw the blood on his arm and touched it.

"You saved me, Zach."

"So we're even."

She smiled and snuggled back against him.

He told her about Simon and Emily being cousins, and how Emily had persuaded Simon to hire Chips Rafferty to hang Ricky. Saying the words hurt him all the more.

"I'm so sorry, Zach. And I know you loved her."

"A long time ago, maybe."

"At least you know the truth of what happened to your

brother. But will she go to prison?"

"For a long, long time."

"I think Simon just didn't know the difference between right and wrong."

"And Fletcher?"

"He knew, but he didn't believe it applied to him." Zach was quiet, impressed by her deep understanding of others, and he could see her bouncing his children on her knees, but maybe she couldn't. Maybe she had only been flirting with him. He had qualms, worries, concerns that she would say no.

For now, he contented himself with holding her in his arms, feeling the warmth and softness, the tickle of her crimson hair against his neck and chin. He tightened his grip now and then to feel her yield to his touch.

He watched for Apache signs, but there were none.

Sunlight spread down the mountain ahead of them, and the rainbow was gone. They could see the Rio Grande, a lazy winding sliver of blue. Sally stirred in his arms.

They could see twenty riders coming from the far side of the river. It was either Luke and his men, or the rest of the outlaws. If they were Rafferty's other men, Zach was in a lot of trouble. He and Sally had been seen, and in a moment, the riders would know who they were.

They sat the saddle a long moment, waiting.

Then Sally straightened. "Is that Luke?"

Far below, Luke reined up with delight. He raised his hat in the air and swung it back and forth. He spun his horse around, then waved his hat once more. Zach was waving his hat in return. Levi was suddenly waving his hat as well.

Up on the hill, Zach was beside himself with joy. Luke was

alive. That meant they had finished off the rustlers, and the Rafferty gang was history. He waved his hat a few more times, then pulled it back on his head.

"See," Sally said, excited. "It's my father and Luke."

"You're right. There ain't no mistakin' a Scofield."

"And what do you mean by that?"

"You're all a pack of trouble."

She twisted in his embrace and smiled up at him. "But you don't really mind, do you?"

"Well, you're awful sassy. I've been wondering what kind of wife you'd make."

"Would you like to find out?"

"Sure would."

"Then your trouble's just starting, Zachariah Lassiter."

"Is that a yes?"

"Yes." She laughed and snuggled closer. "And now maybe you can tell me what your prize was going to be."

"You know dam well it was you."

She giggled. Knowing he had ridden his last lonely trail, he bent his head to kiss her. She would be a heap of trouble, would talk back to him, would never do what she was told, but maybe what she was asked. Their children would be so spirited, they would drive him wild.

And he would love every minute of it.

ABOUT THE AUTHOR

*W*estern novelist and screenwriter **Lee Martin** grew up on cattle ranches in Northern California. Martin began writing in the third grade and, later in life, wrote and sold 43 short stories before turning to novels with 23 now published. Martin is also a prolific writer of screenplays, mostly Westerns.

Martin's screenplay for *Shadow on the Mesa*, starring Kevin Sorbo, Wes Brown, and Gail O'Grady, was based on Martin's novel of the same title (Five Star Publishing, 2014). The movie was the second-highest-rated and second-most-watched original movie in Hallmark Movie Channel's history when it premiered in 2013. The film also won the prestigious Wrangler Award given by the National Cowboy & Heritage Museum in Oklahoma City for Best Original TV Western Movie.

Martin's recent novels, *The Grant Conspiracy*, *The Last Wild Ride*, and *Fury at Cross Creek*, all received rave reviews from *True West Magazine* and were based on Martin's screenplays, as is *Fast Ride to Boot Hill*. *In Mysterious Ways*, Martin's new modern suspense Western, received great critical acclaim from *Kirkus Reviews* and *Midwest Book Reviews*. *Trail of the Fast Gun* is the first book of seven in The Darringer Brothers series, all of which are reissued in paperback and ebook by Vaca Mountain Press.

Martin left the practice of law to write full-time, primarily concentrating on Western screenplays and novels, and often converting one to the other. Several of Martin's screenplays are currently under option by producers. To learn more, visit Lee Martin Westerns on Facebook.

www.ingramcontent.com/pod-product-compliance
Lightning Source LLC
Chambersburg PA
CBHW031238260626

47169CB00007B/2349